# CARNAL KNOWLEDGE

## RACHAEL TAMAYO

**TANGLED TREE**
**PUBLISHING**
tangledtreepublishing.com

CARNAL KNOWLEDGE © 2020 by Rachael Tamayo

Carnal Knowledge is a work of fiction. All names, characters, events and places found therein are either from the author's imagination or used fictitiously. Any similarity to persons alive or dead, actual events, locations, or organizations is entirely coincidental and not intended by the author.

For information, contact the publisher, Tangled Tree Publishing.
WWW.TANGLEDTREEPUBLISHING.COM

EDITING: HOT TREE EDITING
COVER DESIGNER: BOOKSMITH DESIGN
FORMATTING: RMGRAPHX

E-BOOK: ISBN: 978-1-922359-11-7
PAPERBACK: ISBN: 978-1-922359-12-4

# CARNAL KNOWLEDGE

## RACHAEL TAMAYO

A DEADLY SINS NOVEL

For Fred.

# The Sin of Lust

"The most violent appetites in all creatures are lust and hunger; the first is a perpetual call upon them to propagate their kind, the latter to preserve themselves."

—JOSEPH ADDISON

# CHAPTER ONE

## THE RED ROOM

IT ISN'T LONG AFTER I PICK UP MY drink from the table that I feel it. Something is wrong. It's only been one drink; was it extra strong? When did I eat last? My head grows fuzzy and spins, the thumping music in the club sounding far away. I grip the table, struggling to focus as I search the crowd for my friend Lily, but I can't find her. I can't focus on faces. I close my eyes, stumbling on my high heels. I wasn't supposed to be drinking; I figured no one would know as long as I don't drive.

*Where is Lily?* Probably off dancing. She was supposed to be watching my drink.

I stumble again, but this time a strong arm catches me. I catch a whiff of cigarettes, beer, and a strong cologne. *Must be a man.* The thought is vague yet matter-of-fact.

Even as my thinking processes dull and slow, I

realize I'm not drunk. This is something else. This is wrong. I'm too fuzzy to be scared, yet I feel my heart pounding. *I should be afraid.* I didn't come with a man tonight. I don't know any men here. No one should be touching me.

*Don't touch me.*

I try to make my mouth form the words, but I can't. The muscles just won't cooperate. I try to look at him, but my eyes won't focus. My head is just so heavy.

I make out his shape, vague and dark. "Whoa there, beautiful." His voice is laughing and strange. I don't know him, nothing there I recognize.

Is he laughing at me? I don't care. Suddenly so, so sleepy. I open my mouth to speak again, but only slurred, stuttered speech comes out that makes no sense even to my own ears.

He holds me up, leaning close to my ear. "It's okay. I'm not going to let you fall, baby."

\*\*\*

The tears blur my vision, but I can still see the red stain on the floor muddled by the water that drips from my eyes. I drag my hand under my nose, looking at the splattered mess around me. Standing, I stare at the sheets—more red. The blankets are ripped, the sheets half off the bed. The bedside lamp is on the floor. My phone screen is shattered.

Not knowing what else to do, I gather the linens from the bed and walk them down the hall, stuffing them into my washing machine before starting the load. I gather the Clorox bleach spray and a wad of paper towels to clean the wood laminate floor.

It takes a while, but now it looks normal again. The blood is gone. Normal except for the bare mattress and the bleach smell. By this time, I'm almost brave enough to look down. My tears are gone, my vision clear. I've been terrified to look, scared that I'm the source of blood, a wound I can't face or maybe can't feel somewhere that might have caused this mess.

I look down at my body, naked, spattered. I see no cuts, no anything that would suggest blood loss of this magnitude. My head hurts now, so much that I can't concentrate enough to be afraid, or think on what the last thing I remember is, or how I got here, who I might have brought home with me. The answers to the questions that the police would ask, if I were to go to them, which I won't.

Blood is drying on my thighs. I didn't go to bed naked. I don't even remember going to bed or coming home. But that's where I woke up, though I didn't even know I went to sleep, or passed out, or whatever the hell this is. I gingerly touch the back of my head, feeling the growing lump there. My blonde hair feels matted, tangled; it must be the source of the headache.

The blood is mine… I think. The pain I have tells me that at least some of it is probably mine.

I have no idea what happened.

\*\*\*

You really don't know how you feel about some things until they happen to you. You can guess. You can pretend you'd be strong, that you'd stand on the rooftops and shout your indignation as you shake your fist to the skies, but those are only guesses. Hopes. What we think we know about ourselves. They say no one ever really knows anyone. I think it'd be a safe bet to say that we don't really know ourselves either. You think you do. The "Oh, I'd never do that! Look at how she's acting. If I were in her shoes…." but you don't. No one does.

I said the same things to myself when I walked out on my husband, Ricky, months ago. Those thoughts went through my head as I closed the door behind me for what I told myself was the last time. I wouldn't let myself cry as I said goodbye to him, only feeling the first tears fall when I heard the click behind me, the locking of the door to what used to be our home together. When he didn't chase me and beg me to stay.

I wept in that moment, wondering how much pain a person could take.

Over the days that followed, it faded into something more akin to numbness as I found an apartment and got a new checking account. As I arranged to find movers to get my things while he was at work, all while thanking God that we had no children.

Now I find myself in that place once more, though for an altogether different reason. Something has happened to me, something that leaves my body sore and my head feeling as if I have a hangover. These are the moments that tell you who you really are, leaving you exposed to your own darkness.

I found that out about myself. No one ever imagines themselves in this position. You're not prepared. No amount of self-defense can prepare you for the shock that is the next morning, waking up in a bloody mess, knowing you've been sexually assaulted.

I can't even say it out loud. I won't. I refuse to do it. It makes it real, and I don't want it to be real. I want it to be some horrible nightmare that I can wake up from.

But it's not.

It's the middle of the night. I'm sitting on the floor of my shower, the water finally not running pink anymore. My face feels puffy from crying as I carefully wash the wounds, the soap burning. I wince and then stand up before the water turns cold. Sitting here won't accomplish anything.

I look down at the mark on my left breast, swollen and purple. The definite outline of teeth, broken skin, tender to touch. It's not the only place I'm hurting, but it's the only one I can easily see. The only one I can't really hide from. It's a slap in the face, a calling card from someone I can't remember. A face that won't ever haunt my dreams.

So, what do I do now? It's about 4:00 a.m. Do I call someone? The police? My friend Lily? My husband? Maybe Alex? Surely she would believe me.

I blink away tears, dipping my head back into the

hot spray to wash the blood out of my hair.

No, I won't tell anyone. It's too embarrassing. Too humiliating. This big foreboding thing happened to me. What they warned us all about. My drink was tampered with, and someone hurt me. I broke the rules, and I got this for it.

I should have listened, I suppose.

I feel sick knowing what someone did to me while I was asleep. Or was I? Maybe I did fight and just can't remember. I'd fight, surely. I wouldn't just lie there and take it, right? The thought gives me some minimal sliver of peace, like passing through the eye of the hurricane—you know it's not real, not the end, but you relish it just the same.

By the time I get out of the shower, I realize I haven't really slept. My alarm will go off at seven for work so I can catch the bus and be on time for the morning meeting. I could get three hours of sleep before that, maybe.

I shut off the water, suddenly a bit afraid. Knowing someone was here gives me the creeps. Makes me wish I'd gotten that gun Ricky tried so hard to get me to agree to, the one I refused. I wouldn't give in, fearing some horrible accident. He kept his locked up, and I never bothered to learn to shoot. He begged to teach me, tried to get me to hold his Glock to "get the feel of it." Nope. Now I regret it.

In the months I've lived here, I haven't been afraid to be on my own until now. Someone got to me. I'm without defense in my own home.

*Maybe I should get a dog or something.*

I slip the towel over my skin, careful to pat my breast. I rub the towel gently through my hair, mindful of the wound, and then rummage for a bandage. I find something that will do and cover the offending mark with Neosporin, gauze, and tape I have left over after skinning my shins sliding into third at last summer's company softball game.

Back in my room, I cringe, the bare bed terrifying me. I quickly grab a pair of shorts and a shirt and leave the room, shutting the door behind me with a slam. I opt for the couch, with the TV on cartoons and a pillow clutched to my chest. I manage to fall asleep under my granny's handmade afghan with my eyes darting between the door and the TV, wishing for the first time in a while that Ricky was here.

\* \* \*

That was two weeks ago. I only go into my bedroom to change now. I've been sleeping on the couch since that night. Of course, I use the word "sleep" in the loosest terms. Not really sleep, but something akin to it, I suppose. There are dreams, but it's anything but restful. I wake up scared, feeling like someone is watching me and unsure that I slept at all. I know it's because I didn't deal with it, because I'm afraid. That knowledge doesn't help me sleep any better.

I've picked up the phone to call Ricky twice, but

memories of coming home and finding out there was someone else stops me. The imagined visions of him inside another woman trump any fear I have. He let me go, refused to fight for me, and only offered weak apologies. Why would I think he would protect me? Or even care? I always toss the phone aside without calling.

I almost think maybe I need to tell someone; I even try to work up the courage to tell Lily, but I just can't be sure that she wouldn't blame me, or tell everyone, or even stop calling me altogether to hang out. We work together—she's a paralegal in the law firm where I work as an assistant to one of the partners—and she's nice, but we just aren't that close, so dropping a bomb like this on her just doesn't seem to fit.

She's the one who dragged me out, insisting I needed to get out of the house. The next day after it happened, when she asked me where I went, I told her I couldn't find her and figured she'd met someone, so I went home.

"I assumed the same thing. We've got to be more careful." She wagged her finger at me, using a mock fatherly tone, and we both giggled.

I laughed then, didn't know what else to do. I felt like such an idiot. I thought I'd been careful.

It was then that I decided that I needed to just forget about it, tuck it away. Live in denial. I don't know what happened, and I never will. The mark is gone, and I can forget now.

I don't think denial is such a bad place to live.

# CHAPTER TWO

## PRETEND IT NEVER HAPPENED

"HEY, WREN, HOT STUFF WANTS TO SEE you," Lily hisses through the door of my cubicle.

I look up into her green eyes and find she's stifling a laugh. Hot Stuff is what she likes to call Doug Larson. He's the newest and youngest senior partner at forty-seven. Handsome for his age, and the rumors fly around the office about him and his prowess with the ladies—tales that he's dipped his pen into the company ink, if you know what I mean. I know better than to believe rumors, but sometimes that's easier said than done.

"Why?" I glance at the clock—almost two.

"I don't know. I was just in there, and he said to send you in. Maybe he wants you to take dictation." She laughs.

I smile, offering a chuckle. "You're so dirty." I stand up, slipping my high heels back onto my feet.

"I know, but he really is hot for an old guy, don't

you think?"

"He's not old."

She shrugs. "He's old enough."

"True."

Mr. Larson's office is huge, of course, all glass and metal, cold yet beautiful. The click of my heels on the hard floor of the hall is silenced by thick, plush carpet once I cross the threshold. I close the door and glance around. He's not at his desk, a monstrous thing with distressed dark wood surrounded by matching suede furniture. It smells like leather, a scent I love, but in here it somehow always makes me antsy.

"Wren, do you want a drink?" I hear him ask.

A drink? I stifle a scoff, finding him at a hideaway bar of sorts in the far corner. He's pouring something clear from a decanter over ice.

"No, thank you." I've got a drug and alcohol test with my probation officer this afternoon. But he doesn't know that.

He turns his blue eyes my way, smiling. "You sure?" A handsome man, no doubt. A man with money and taste. I bet no one ever tells him no. A man who knows how to get his way, who's good at what he does, and the women fall all over him. He's all these things in my imagination, of course; in real life, I have no idea. He could be some blundering, clumsy nerd for all I know.

I don't sit since I wasn't asked to. Doug walks up to me, drink in hand, eyes on me. He takes a sip, then sets it on the desk. His hand is cool from the glass when he touches my elbow. "My dear, I have a proposal for you. Next week I'm going to a conference for three days, and I need an assistant while I'm there. It's in San Francisco. I'd like you to come with me—all expenses paid, of course. And you'd be working, so I'd pay you twenty-four hours a day while we're there."

*Oh crap.* I swallow, wishing I had that drink right about now. A trip with him. Now, I need the money. And how bad could it be, really? The five bucks I have in my bank account could really use the company. Maybe he's not like they say. Even if he is, surely I could avoid letting anything happen, right?

But what if he got mad? If I get fired, I could go to jail. Having a job is a condition of my probation. But maybe he's really a cool guy, who knows? Who cares if he's forty-seven and I'm only twenty-six? There's also the fact that maybe he really does just want me there to work, considering the type of women I've seen him go for in the past—thin, classy, beautiful. I don't quite fit the bill in my size twelve suit. A tight twelve at that. Sure, maybe I have a pretty face, but still. Of course, there's also the sexual harassment thing. The ace in my back pocket, just in case he was to try something. But when you really think about it, how often does that "If you want your job, you'll give me what I want" ultimatum happen outside of old eighties TV shows?

"Um, next week?"

He nods, his hand drifting from my elbow down to my hand. "Yes, starting Monday. We leave Sunday night, get back sometime Thursday. Depending on how it goes, I could give you the rest of the week off, paid." I look up into his eyes. He licks his thin lips and holds my gaze. "Do you have a reason why you can't go?"

"Um, no, no I don't." I need my job. I need the money. Not enough to sleep with him, but I can avoid that, I'm sure. I doubt any of the rumors are true anyway. I'm most likely just jumping to conclusions, my brain going into full-on paranoia mode after two weeks of no sleep.

His smile is broad. "Good. We'll get together Saturday for dinner to discuss the details before the trip. I'll pick you up." He winks at me.

"Yes, sir," I agree softly, then leave his office.

As soon as I get to my desk, I start to message Lily, who I heard slept with him before—even though I know she doesn't know I know. Of course, I don't even know if it's true. Then I think better of it, slide the phone aside, and try to get back to work.

\* \* \*

Alex is my probation officer. She's in her midthirties, I think, though I can't be sure based on looks alone. She's on the phone, motioning for me to sit down in the chair by her desk, a Naugahyde thing that probably came with the office when she got the position. Her long, loose, dark hair falls into her face, hiding chocolate brown eyes as she bends to the left to pull out a clear plastic cup with a yellow lid in a sealed plastic bag.

She hands it to me, her bronze skin stark in comparison to my pale hand when I lean forward and take it from her. She points to the bathroom across the hall and then keeps talking as I stand up.

I think she's supposed to watch me, but she hasn't since the first time, thank God. Nothing quite compares to having someone you hardly know watch you pee.

I walk out and into the bathroom. It's small with only three stalls and one of those wall things that sprays air freshener at timed intervals, so it smells of vanilla or some other generically pleasant odor. I manage to fill the cup and not get any on me, then head back to the office. She's off the phone now, and I set the deposit on the corner of her desk. With a smile, she labels it, seals it up, and puts it on the desk behind her. I assume I'm supposed to see her do this so I can't accuse her of tampering with it or something.

"How are you, Wren?" She pulls out a form, tapping a pen on the table as she meets my eye. Her voice is rough, sultry even. Sort of like Kathleen Turner from movies I used to watch as a kid. *Romancing the Stone* and all that.

"I'm doing okay. Nothing special." I shrug.

"Being a good girl?" she teases with a wink, standing. "Come with me."

"Of course. I'm an angel." I snort.

She glances over her shoulder, laughing lightly as if she knows what I mean. As if she's no angel herself.

I know where we're going as I follow her out of the

office and down the hall, then through an unmarked door to an Intoxilyzer—the kind of machine the police use to check your alcohol level.

"You know the drill," she states.

Of course I pass. 0.00.

We head back to the office, where she signs the form, and I watch her send my pee down the hall for a drug test.

"When am I supposed to come back?" I shoulder my purse and watch her grab her planner from the corner of the desk, turning pages with medium-length manicured nails in a bright blue.

"Um, I have you down for the tenth. I expect everything will come back fine, so I won't call you unless there's a problem. Behave, and call me if you need me." She turns her attention to the computer.

Time for me to go.

"Thanks. See you next time, Alex."

As I walk out, my phone goes off. I fish it out of the side pocket on my purse to find that Lily is texting me.

**Lily: Hey, my old college roommate is having a big party tonight. You have to come with me. I don't want to look like a loser going alone.**

**Me: You going to abandon me this time?** Seems like I could get away with a party since I just took my drug and alcohol test. Maybe a drink or two won't hurt me this time.

Lily: No, not unless you want me to. She knows some hot guys.

Me: Hot guys? But it's a work night. We have to be up early.

Lily: So? Don't get drunk, dummy. And yes, hot guys. You're coming with me.

I haven't even thought about men like that since…. I shake it away. I won't let it get to me. I decide not to remember that I still don't sleep in my bed. Even before that happened, I didn't dare to step out into the dating world. Being unsure of myself after Ricky's indiscretion, plus still feeling married and like I would be doing something wrong, always stopped the thoughts dead in their tracks.

But you're supposed to get back on the horse, right? Back in the saddle, so to speak.

\*\*\*

Hours later, in a big house full of strangers, Lily urges me toward every hot guy she sees. I sip on a very weak rum and Coke and remind myself that she has no idea what happened to me only two weeks ago. When she asks me why I'm not drinking more, I make excuses, mostly reminding her that we work tomorrow. She downs her second, then a third, and I wonder if I'll end up taking her home.

Turning, meaning to find a place to set my empty glass, I end up getting my foot crunched under someone's boot.

"Ow!" I shout, figuring the music covers me anyway. Only then do I look up at a wall of a body.

"Shit, I'm sorry. Are you okay?" asks a deep, apologetic voice. A voice I know. A voice that speaks to something deep inside me. His familiar scent, spicy and warm, evokes memories that draw my eyes up to see if it really is who I think it is.

Our eyes meet at the same time, and silence falls between us. Ricky. My husband. He has on the Mötley Crüe T-shirt I got for him, nice jeans, and heavy boots that just crushed my now throbbing left foot. He has on his wedding ring, which shocks me more than the fact that I'm looking at him for the first time since I walked out. He's sober and standing alone. His eyes are clear and bright, shining a sharp gray. His hair is longer, shaggy and light brown. It looks good, suits him. I always loved it when he wore his hair like this.

"Ricky." His name comes out soft, almost erotic, though I don't mean for it to. "What are you doing here?"

He looks me over slowly. "Killing time, mostly." He shrugs. "Buck invited me to come hang out, so here I am."

Buck. Not a bad guy, one of his oldest friends. *Is he here to meet a woman? Does he have a girlfriend? Did they break up? Is she waiting back at home for him? In my home? Did he move her in?* Questions race through my mind, along with confusing emotions. Words seem

17

to get stuck in my mouth. It's odd to look at the face of a man you know so well and be at a loss for words.

"What are you doing here?" he asks, filling the silence when I don't.

"Oh, I came with Lily."

My mind flashes back to that night, which is when I got my DWI. I was so hurt and angry that I stopped and got drunk, then got behind the wheel. I backed into a parked police cruiser in the parking lot of the bar across the street from the hotel I was going to stay at. My first and only arrest, and I still blame him. He drove me to become the worst part of myself.

"Lily?" He furrows his brow, but then recognition seems to fill his eyes. "Oh, I remember her. From your office."

I nod, shoving my hands into my back pockets. I want to know about *her*, but I can't ask. I don't want to hear the answers. "Yeah. She dragged me out."

"You work tomorrow, don't you?"

I nod, and he smirks at me. "Come with me. I'll get you a drink."

He offers his hand to me, but I stare at it as if it's a trap. Do I take it? Does it mean anything? What will it feel like to touch him again? I swallow, looking into his eyes. Is he conflicted too? Confused? Does he still love me?

Do I still love him?

I finally take his hand. It feels the same, familiar, gentle, hot. Home. He's still home. It gives me a twisted sense of peace to touch him again. To be dragged carefully behind him through the crowd at a party toward a bar. To be handed an open beer, my favorite, because he knows me. I haven't gone for a divorce yet, haven't been able to bring myself to do it. I don't know why I'm biding my time. Maybe I can't bring myself to let go, to believe it. I married him at twenty. For six years, he was my world. I adored him. Even when he pulled away, I made excuses to myself. Walking out the door on him was the hardest thing I ever did. Now I'm standing in the middle of a stranger's kitchen drinking a beer with him.

*What the hell am I doing?*

The beer is ice cold. It's good, and I fill my mouth with it, then lick it off my lips before taking another sip. He's watching me; I feel his eyes. I look up and see a quiet smile, the silent words in his eyes, and wonder if I see what's really there or simply what my heart wants to see.

"I'd like to talk," he says. "Can we?"

\* \* \*

She was young, maybe twenty. Maybe not. Her brown hair was pulled into a tight ponytail that was quite long, telling me her hair was probably almost to her waist. With a look of indignation on her face and fear in her eyes, she stood on my doorstep, staring at me. I had no idea who she was.

I smiled, leaning on the doorframe.

"Can I help you?"

She glanced around, then back to me. A deep breath puffed up her ample chest. "Um, are you Wren, Ricky's wife?"

I nodded. "I am. Is there something wrong?"

She clutched her shoulder bag tightly with one trembling hand. "Yes, something is wrong. He… I…."

\* \* \*

I snap back to the present, freshly angered by the memory. Recalling what she told me on my doorstep, seeing him pull up in his truck and seeing his face through the windshield, staring at us before getting out slowly and just standing there, staring at me. Mouthing "I'm so sorry" to me.

"Can we talk?" I echo. "No."

I turn, walking away from him with tears in my eyes, ashamed of how I still feel for him. Wishing I could hate him yet knowing I never really can. Loathing the fact that I want him back, along with my life, those moments with him that created days that built into weeks and months and years.

But no. No life with the man I chose for me. No, ma'am.

I hear his voice behind me, calling me, but I keep walking. It's not until I reach the front porch that he stops me with a gentle grip on my arm.

"Let me go," I say without turning.

"We have to talk at some point."

I don't look at him. Instead, I pull my arm away and fish my phone out of my pocket, telling Lily that I need to leave. I call for an Uber and tell Ricky I'm going home. I won't talk to him. What is there to say? Another "I'm sorry"? That it was a mistake? Some stupid excuse?

He releases a swear, blown out on a breath, then goes back inside, leaving me alone on the porch.

I sit down on the stoop, glad no one is with me. I don't feel like explaining what it's like to hate someone you love so much.

# CHAPTER THREE

## AGAIN

*THE KIND OF BLACKNESS THAT DROWNS* swallows me. Heavy eyelids, so heavy I can't open them. The crushing feeling of being pressed into the mattress, held down, something wet dribbling on my skin. I try to scream, try to lash out, but I can't. So, so heavy.

I think it's a dream when I wake up. What else would it be? Curled in blankets, sweating, I realize I'm late for work and bolt out of bed, shaming myself for going out on a work night. I didn't stay, but I was up half the night, upset over seeing Ricky again. I forgot to set my alarm, I guess.

Dashing for the shower, it isn't until after I've washed my hair, that I look down and see it. I want to scream, but my throat locks up. I want to run, but I can't run from myself, so I just stand there, my chest heaving as I stare down at this thing that laughs at me and brings water to my eyes and a whimper to my throat.

How could this be possible?

A fresh bite mark, same breast. Same broken skin, same bruising. Fuck. Tears burn my eyes as I touch it, wincing. It hurts, a lot. I reach into my mind for anything and find only the dream. The dream of being crushed in the dark.

He came back.

It wasn't a dream.

I rinse off and wrap a towel around my still-dripping hair, then head into my bedroom. No blood this time. Last night was the first time I dared to try to sleep in here, telling myself that I was silly to be so scared.

And now here I am.

I wonder if someone is watching me. How else could he know that I slept in here last night? He couldn't, right? Just a coincidence. Nothing strange, nothing out of place. Grabbing another towel, I start to rub it over my hair as I walk around the apartment. The door is locked, as are the windows. No one has a key to my apartment but me.

What on earth happened? I wasn't even drunk last night. This can't be reality, can it? But someone *is* watching me. It's the only answer.

Not knowing what to do, what to think, I dress as I cry. How could it have happened again? How could he do something like this to me and not even wake me up?

As I change, I look down at my body again, checking

for anything that might be wrong, different. The bruise is so tiny, I would have missed it. Right in the crook of my arm. A needle mark. He got me again.

Shit, what did he give me? Was it the same as last time?

I start to shake as I pick up my blouse and slip it on. Cool satin over my skin. I feel fine, no hint of a hangover of any sort this time. Whatever it was, it wore off fast.

Would anyone even believe me if I called someone? Lily? The police? Who does someone talk to about something like this? *Hey, I had a bad dream and then woke up with this*. They would laugh me out of the police station.

I wish my mom were here. She would know what to do.

I stand in my kitchen, thinking and arguing with myself. What is the next most logical step that won't make me a laughingstock?

I've got to get an alarm for my door or something, maybe change my locks. That should do it, right?

*If it happens again, I will tell someone*, I promise myself. Setting my orange juice glass on the counter, I look around, making plans. I'll take a long lunch today and go to Home Depot to get some kind of alarm for my door, something I can afford that isn't a monthly subscription. At least it'll make noise and scare him off.

As I walk out the door, I struggle not to wonder,

*Did he do it again? Was I sexually assaulted a second time?* I don't feel anything strange, not sore or bruised.

I shake it away, refusing to let the idea sink in.

But then why would he come back?

\*\*\*

I walk out of Home Depot with this little thingy that sticks to a door or window and will sound an alarm if it's opened. I got one for the front door, all my windows, and even my bedroom door. I feel better as I get into the back of the Uber to head back to work, grateful the driver is a woman since I'm a bit shy of strangers right now. I called the front office when they opened, and my locks are being changed while I'm at work today. Everything should be okay.

An hour after I return to the office, I'm elbow deep in my to-do pile when Doug walks into my cubicle and plops down in my little chair. I look up, surprised that he came to me instead of vice versa.

I stop typing and try to smile. "Mr. Larson, what can I do for you?"

"Wren, I'm right in the middle of ten things, and I was hoping you might do me a little favor this afternoon." His bright blue eyes smile, almost twinkling at me, standing out against his tanned skin and his dark brown hair. He has to know he's handsome, right? Knows women think so. Hell, I think so, and he's quite a bit older than I am.

"What would that be?"

He leans forward and puts his keys on the desk in front of me. "I need you to take my car to the shop. It's acting up. I'll send an Uber to pick you up."

I stare at his keys, unsure of what to do. I'm not supposed to be driving, but I'd rather risk it than have anyone here find out. I don't want to deal with the stares or lose my job over one stupid mistake. "Um… yeah, sure. Send the info to my phone."

A few minutes later, I slide into a luxury vehicle that I would never be able to afford. It's been a few months since I got behind the wheel of a car. I sit in his BMW, the soft leather cradling my butt. The scent of his cologne is on everything in here, and while not an unpleasant smell at all, I roll down the window anyway. Fresh air hits my face, and I breathe it in.

I pull out of the parking garage, careful to look both ways.

It happens out of nowhere. I don't see it coming, just feel it.

Sudden impact, pain, the crash of metal, broken glass. My head hurts. Blood drips into my eyes. My vision blurs. God, my head hurts.

*No, no, no, no, no. That didn't just happen.*

I throw the car door open, noting the steam—or is it smoke?—coming from the crumpled hood of my boss's car. Shit. Head-on collision. The opposing vehicle fared better, being a huge pickup truck. The driver gets out as I try to stand up but fail, tumbling to the hot pavement and skinning my knee.

"Shit, are you okay? God, I'm so sorry." The woman falls to her knees beside me, touching my head with one hand and dialing 911 with the other. I want to stop her, tell her not to call, but I can't focus enough to get the words out of my mouth.

All I can think of is the fact that my boss will fire me, and I'm going to end up in jail for violating my probation.

Sirens. Flashing lights and heavy boots on concrete. Paramedics offering soft words of comfort as they put gentle pressure on the bleeding. An officer scribbles down my information just as the medics load me into the back of an ambulance despite my protests.

I need to make phone calls.

Then the world goes black.

\* \* \*

I wake in the hospital. The light is bright, even through drawn curtains. It peeks around the edges and illuminates the room. I'm lying in a bed, blanket covering me, bandage on my head. I look around and see a heavyset woman in scrubs messing with my IV, pushing buttons.

Why am I here? I struggle to sit up, my head heavy, suddenly throbbing. I moan out a strange noise and she turns to me, offering a frown, telling me to take it easy. Calling me sweetie.

"What happened?"

"You have a mild concussion. Your memory might be a bit…"

As she's talking, adjusting me, I remember. The crash, my boss's car now crumpled, the ambulance, everything. I groan, suddenly feeling heavy.

Then panic sets in. I crashed his car. What if he fires me? What if Alex finds out? She could send me to prison for violating my probation. I've worked at this firm for about three years now. Plus, what if they find out that I have a DWI? The whole thing happened that weekend, after that woman showed up on my doorstep. A three-day weekend that thankfully kept my coworkers from finding out what had happened. Lily doesn't even know. When she asked me, I told her my car broke down and it cost so much to fix that I decided not to mess with it, and I couldn't afford a car payment now that I was on my own. She bought it. Why wouldn't she?

I come back to reality. Concussion. Memory loss, headaches, take it easy, don't move too fast, nausea—I pick up all the keywords while I try to look like I know what's going on and that I'm paying attention. Between strangers drugging me, my husband, and now this, I don't have much room left in my brain.

But her next words catch my full attention. "We called your husband. He's on his way."

Shit. They called Ricky. He's still my emergency contact. That's one of those little details you don't really think to change. Damn it. I can't fault them, but now I have—

The door bursts open and he stands there for a moment, eyes darting back and forth. He's pale and wearing khaki pants and a polo shirt with the police academy logo on the pocket. I am surprised not to see him in his patrol uniform, but then again, it's been so long since we spoke that I'm not surprised to find myself clueless. Wild eyes settle on me, and a visible relief passes over his features as he steps in, letting the door close behind him. "What happened? They only told me you were in an accident and had a head injury. Are you okay? I left as soon as I could."

I look at him as he approaches the edge of my bed. He touches my head gingerly, so lightly I hardly feel it except for how his fingertips brush my forehead. "What happened?" he asks again.

The nurse walks out without saying anything else, leaving me with him.

"My boss asked me to take his car to the shop, and I got into an accident," I explain. "She said I have a concussion."

"Damn. How do you feel?"

I look up into worried gray eyes. "I don't know yet. I'm still feeling a little fuzzy."

The nurse walks back in. "Ma'am, I forgot to tell you that the police are here to speak with you. The detective has been waiting for you to wake up."

Detective? Police? That sense of foreboding comes

back, and I look at Ricky, who has a frown and a furrowed brow. At one time, his disapproval would have hurt me very much. His frown, the way he would shake his head and look away, would have had me rushing to find a way to show him that I wasn't the disappointment that he surely thought I was. Not now. That's gone. He's the cause of the damn thing, so why would I care? I never would have drunk like that and then been so stupid if not for what he did.

I thank the nurse and then look away from him, pretending to examine my hospital bracelet, adjust my blankets.

"Why is a detective here?"

I shrug. I hope it's not because I drove without a valid license. I doubt they would send a detective for that. "I guess we'll find out."

It isn't long before someone's knocking on the door, opening it before I have a chance to reply. Ricky has taken the only chair in the room, having dragged it to my bedside. A large, round man who looks close to fifty steps inside the room with a gun belt on, handcuffs dangling. He wears dress pants and a shirt and tie, his badge on his belt, shiny gold against the black leather. "Pardon me. I'm Detective Martin Small. I was hoping to speak to you for a moment." He pulls out a card and hands it to me.

"Sure. What is this about?"

His eyes dart to my companion.

"I'm sure you probably know Ricky. I don't care if

he's here for whatever this is." I sigh, suddenly tired.

The men shake hands. "Hey, Ricky. Good to see you, I was sorry to see you quit. How is the academy treating you?" The detective nods at him, then pulls out a little notepad and a pen as he speaks

Ricky glances at me, aware that I don't know. That I will have questions. Assuming anyway, assuming that I care. "Oh, thanks. I appreciate that. It was a rough decision to make, but I think for now, I'm better suited to teaching our future boys in blue than actually being one. Maybe in the future I can come back."

So he quit. I wonder what happened. I don't ask, just turn my attention back to the detective. He looks away from Ricky with a sobering, serious expression on his face.

"Mrs. Addison." He turns to me. "The hospital staff called me because they were concerned that you'd been assaulted due to a mark on your person. They discovered it during your exam in the emergency room and stated that it wasn't caused by your accident today." He isn't asking me a question but stops talking and waits regardless, as if he's expecting something from me.

I breathe in and out, deliberate and slow. *Stay calm. They know; they saw it.*

Ricky is now sitting up in his seat, paying attention.

He goes on when I don't respond. "The mark in question is a bite mark on your chest. It's infected and pretty fresh, they told me. Can you tell me what happened? Did someone do this to you? Was it consensual?"

I sit up too fast, sparking a dull thud in the back of my head. "It most certainly was not! Why would I consent to being bitten like this?" I remark.

He shows no emotion, no reaction. A face of stone. "Mrs. Addison, I don't like to make presumptions about people's extracurricular activities. I make no judgment. Were you assaulted?" He pulls out his phone and proceeds to show me a picture of the bite on my chest. As if I'd never seen it before. I bite back a comment on the fact that he felt the need to shove a picture in my face, wishing that I'd kicked Ricky out of here. I assume it was taken by someone in the ER. *What happened to HIPAA laws? Can they even do that without my permission?* I swallow, knowing my emotions are misplaced, that it really doesn't matter.

Ricky stands, peering over between us, then looks up at me.

"What the fuck is this?"

I guess my emotions aren't the only ones that are misplaced.

"It's a bite mark," I say quietly, barely reining in my sarcasm.

He looks at the detective, incredulous. "What the hell happened here? Someone bit my wife?"

Suddenly I'm his wife again? I almost laugh at that one.

"That's what I'm trying to find out," he says coolly.

I lie back, unsure of what to say. I suppose the truth. But laying all that out isn't something I expected to do. I could lie, but I've never been much of a liar; I can't keep my story straight, and my face always gives me away.

"Yes, someone did assault me, but I don't know who," I say after a long moment.

Both men stare at me, one flatly, scribbling, and the other with his mouth gaping open.

After a deep breath, I tell them what happened, both two weeks ago and this morning. I show Small the needle mark in my arm. After I get it all out, I pull the covers up higher, hoping it'll hide me from Ricky's pissed-off, indignant, "why didn't you tell me" glare, but it doesn't. He closes his mouth and sits down heavily, his head in one hand.

"I presume you didn't see a doctor two weeks ago for the sexual assault," Small asks. I shake my head. "I need to have a rape kit done on you, just in case." It's not a question.

I wonder if I can decline, but I know better than to try. I just nod, not speaking.

"I appreciate your honesty, ma'am. I'm going to write up a report. I'll order the rape kit, and we'll be in touch. If something else happens, or you think of anything, you can call me at that number." He points to the card I set on the side table.

"Thank you."

"Martin, can I talk to you in the hall?" Ricky stands

up, ready to follow him out. Small nods, letting him lead the way.

My curiosity is almost enough to get me out of bed to open the door and intrude on their conversation, so obviously about me. I sit up and mute the TV, straining to hear, hoping they might be just outside the door.

Now I wish I'd asked Ricky to leave. I don't know what I was thinking. I should have made him go. Damn it.

The door opens only moments later, and Ricky comes back alone, looking upset if not full-on angry. "What the ever-loving fuck, Wren?" He's not yelling, but there's a surprising amount of pain in his words. He doesn't look at me, instead leaning back in the chair after he sits down, casting his gaze heavenward. "You were sexually assaulted two weeks ago? Why—"

"Why didn't I tell you? You can't possibly be so stupid as to ask me that question. You haven't been a part of my life for months. Why would I call you?"

"We're still married. You think I don't care? You think I wouldn't show up to protect you? Help you? Come on." He looks at me now, and it hurts. Staring into eyes that I loved, that I still love, and that hurt me so terribly still stings.

"Why would I want you to? After what you did?" My voice starts to quiver, but I steady it. "How can you think that I'd just pick up the phone and tell you something like that?" I whisper, my emotion having stolen my voice.

"Wren, I'm sorry. You won't talk to me about it. I want to talk to you, try to explain. But whatever happens, even if we don't ever talk about it, I'll always be here for you. When you need something, anything, call me."

"You got a woman pregnant." I say it calmly, as flatly as the detective. I'm proud of the tone my voice carries. I sound strong. Unaffected. He probably knows I'm not, but I don't care.

"I told you she wasn't pregnant. She was lying." He locks his eyes on me, a silent plea. An unspoken "I am so sorry."

I turn away, reaching around for the remote, turning on the television.

"Oh, well, then perhaps I owe you an apology on that account. She lied about being pregnant. I assume the fact that you came inside her is forgivable, then?"

He looks toward the ceiling, muttering something I can't make out before saying, "Don't be a smart-ass."

"I have every right. Why are you here? I don't need you."

"Well, I'm not leaving." He sets his eyes on the screen as I flip through bad hospital cable. "And if you think you're going home to that apartment alone, you're insane."

I stare at him, but he doesn't look at me. I could argue, tell him he can't tell me what to do, but my head aches and I'm too tired, so I lie back and settle on an episode of *Friends*.

When my phone rings, I'm mostly asleep. I barely stir as I hear the dreamy voice of Ricky answering, telling them I'm asleep. Then my eyes pop open. Wide awake. "Why did you answer my phone?"

He turns to me. "Why are you on probation?"

I swallow. Well, the cat's out of the bag now. Isn't this just peachy. "I asked you first." I cross my arms. How long was I asleep? I grab the phone, realizing it's almost seven in the evening.

"I didn't know it was off-limits. Your turn."

"You can't expect me to believe that one of your buddies didn't call you when I got arrested. That you didn't go into work the next day and get an earful from ten people about how your drunk wife was busted for DWI. You know exactly why. And that leads me to believe that you laid there in bed after they called you, knowing I was in jail, and just rolled over and went back to sleep. You didn't do a damn thing. So don't stand there all high and mighty, thinking you're going to fool me into feeling like you're catching me at something." I cross my arms over my chest with finality. "I don't know when you quit the department, but it sure as shit wasn't that day. I'd just left."

He just stares, unwavering. I can't tell if it's accusing or not. I'm not the type to go out drinking and then drive. Way out of my character. Internally I debate between stubbornly remaining silent and pretending as if his actions didn't devastate me to the point that it changed who I was, even if for a moment, and just giving in and telling the truth. Opening the door to that conversation isn't something that sounds good to me right now, so I opt for silence and indignation instead.

He sighs, long and loud. "Look, I get it. I know what I did was bad. Worse than bad. But I—"

"Please don't. I'm tired, and I can't do this right now." My voice is hushed. "I'm in the hospital, for God's sake."

A flicker of shame crosses his eyes before he looks back at the TV and leaves it alone. I release a breath, half wishing he would go home and half happy not to be here alone. I know that eventually we will have to talk, but not now.

I fall asleep, but there isn't much rest in it. I get woken up by nurses, by my own strangely vivid dreams, and the dull throb in my head. Ricky sleeps on a chair that pulls out into a bed, with a flat hospital pillow under one of those thin blue blankets. He snores lightly, and the sound confuses my soul. I never realized how it used to lull me to sleep until I had to learn to sleep without it. Now it gives me a twisted peace, as if it's something I've been missing.

He's just familiar. Ricky can't be my home; if he was, he wouldn't have done what he did.

Morning comes, along with breakfast. Right after the nurse shows up with a meal, Ricky returns from the deli on the corner with food and coffee just how I like it.

"Thanks." I mean it.

He nods, sitting down without saying anything.

The morning drags as we wait for an update from the doctor. I'm surprised Ricky remains by my side, at one point calling his boss and stepping into the hallway to explain what's going on. He tells me that he'll stay as long as he needs to, and he won't hear an argument.

I don't know how to feel.

It doesn't help when a doctor and a nurse come in, rolling a cart. They look at Ricky with solemn, uncomfortable eyes. "We need to perform an exam. Can you…?"

Ricky stands up. "Sure, sure. I'll go get some coffee or something." He looks back at me but leaves without saying another word.

"I'm Doctor Sharma, and this is Nurse Day. The police have ordered a forensic sexual assault exam. We're here to perform the exam and take evidence."

I nod, not sure what else to do. It's not really a time for conversation.

They go over every inch of me, swabbing my mouth, combing my hair and taking the loose ones into a bag. Anything that falls on the collection drape they placed under me is collected. I'm poked and prodded within an inch of my life. The whole process is embarrassing, invasive, and humiliating.

"You have some minor tearing in your vaginal canal. It looks new, so I would say this is fresh and not from the first assault that the police mentioned in their evidence request. I would take it easy, avoid any further sexual activity for a few weeks to allow it to heal," Doctor Sharma says, covering me back up. "The exam is complete. You did well, considering the circumstances. The police will collect the evidence."

"Okay. Thanks." *Yeah, thanks for violating me so completely and politely. Thanks for confirming the fact that I was raped—again.* This is bullshit. No woman should have to deal with this.

They file out, and I'm left alone with my emotions once again. I turn toward the hospital TV, unseeing.

# CHAPTER FOUR

## PISSING CONTEST

THE DAY WEARS INTO AFTERNOON. I FALL asleep and take a nap, and the two of us finally settle into something that isn't just painful and awkward. I need to call Alex back, but I put it off. At lunch, Ricky goes to Freebirds and brings me back a burrito and a Coke, telling me that I don't have to eat the hospital food.

Back when we were together, he would cook. It was one of the things I really enjoyed about him. He would sit me down with a wink and then disappear, and the house would fill with the lovely smell of whatever he was cooking. Sometimes he would barbeque, even in winter. I smile, remembering how he would bundle up in the freezing cold and stand over the pit, flipping burgers and roasting corn.

"What?" he asks.

"What?"

"You're sitting there grinning." He smiles at me.

"Was I? Oh, it's nothing." I shrug, pulling more foil off my burrito. He doesn't need to know why I was smiling.

"You don't have to be this way."

"What way?" I take a bite as I feign ignorance. The food is flavorful and hot, just how I like it.

"Cold, distant. Pretending like you don't care. This isn't you." He dips a chip into nacho cheese sauce, and it crunches loudly when he bites it.

He's right. It's not me, but he made it me. The argument stands: did he turn me into something I'm not, or did the pain simply bring out a side that was there all along?

Someone knocks, pulling me from the thought. I call for them to come in and then the door opens, saving me from further interrogation. I expect the doctor but instead see my boss, Doug. He has food bags in one hand, a fast food cup in the other. He glances between me and Ricky, his face revealing nothing. "Oh, hello. I guess someone else beat me to feeding you." He flashes his white teeth at us.

"Hey, I'm Enrique." Ricky walks around the bed and offers a hand to Doug.

I scoff internally. He almost never uses his given name. It's always Ricky.

"Hi. I'm Wren's boss. How are you?" He shakes the massive hand and watches me, directing the question to me instead of Ricky.

"I'm awful, thanks. Hey, Mr. Larson, about your car—"

He sets the food down and rushes to my side, taking my hand between his. I want to pull away but know the delicate situation I'm in, so I don't. "Wren, dear, stop. The car isn't important. I'm just so glad that you're being taken care of. They're taking care of you, aren't they?"

"Yes. I'll be released tomorrow, I think. It's a concussion, so I can't work for a few—"

"Stop, don't worry about that. You just rest. Let me know what you need, and I'll take care of it."

"I'm Wren's husband," Ricky says, unsmiling, interrupting and obviously jealous of my attention, however innocent it may be.

I bristle. "Estranged, soon-to-be ex-husband," I correct. "Don't forget that part."

Doug's eyebrows go up, while Ricky turns to me and just shakes his head.

"Come on, little bird," he says after a moment, moving to my side.

Little bird. He hasn't called me that in so very long. A pet name he gave me back when we were dating, a few months in. The first time we had sex, I remember him lying beside me, up on his elbow with soft eyes, brushing my hair from my face. Looking into my eyes and whispering it to me with love in his voice and dancing in his gaze.

He has the same look now, love lighting up his face.

I open my mouth, then close it again. I don't know what I was going to say. Instead of replying, I turn to Doug and tell him to sit down, knowing Ricky's trying to make Doug uncomfortable so he'll leave. Doug sets the food down on the table, and I ask him how work is. We talk about what's going on, about his car, and so on. Ricky stands, arms crossed over his broad chest, watching in silence, brooding with a frown that droops by the minute. Doug mentions the conference, and I tell him that I'll probably still be fine to go with him.

I don't expect Doug to stay long, but he does. He and Ricky talk about sports a little and this and that, crap men talk about when they don't know each other but are trying to fill dead air with their own voices. We all watch TV for a bit, and after a while I start to realize that they're in a pissing contest. They're outwaiting one another, each hoping the other will leave first.

I need to get Doug out of here. It's getting uncomfortable being caught between them both, and frankly I'm just tired. I lie back and sigh. "My head hurts."

Ricky stands up and moves over to me. "Want your nurse, baby?"

The sound of that rough voice calling me "baby," even if I know it's for Doug's sake, confuses my heart a little. I should laugh at him and end this charade. He might as well pee on me to mark me as his and call it a day.

"Please. I could use some pain meds." I want to tell him not to call me that, but I bite it back. I don't want to fight in front of someone else.

He bends, touching his lips to mine. Soft, gentle. "Push your call button. I'll go get you some water." He grabs my cup and winks at me as he heads out the door.

He kissed me. What the hell? My lips burn, as does my heart, and confusion washes over me along with the heat that's surely turned my cheeks a rich and embarrassing shade of crimson.

Doug doesn't look too happy just before Ricky walks out. I can almost see him trying not to roll his eyes.

The nurse pops right in and offers me meds, then tells me that the doctor is headed my way to talk to me.

Ricky comes back in and flashes a smile and a hello at the nurse as she walks out. "Here you go."

I gingerly take the cup from him. "Thank you."

He pets my head, pushing my hair back, then kisses my forehead. His eyes give away the mischief on his mind, and we both look at Doug, who's frowning.

I'd say mission accomplished.

What a jackass.

Eventually the doctor comes in, and Doug finally says his goodbyes.

"Well, how are you feeling? I see you've eaten."

I nod. "Right now, I'm all right. Eating seemed to help."

He nods, checking my eyes before he sits down.

"Well, you can go home tomorrow. Tonight, the nurse will be in to wake you every few hours to make sure you can wake up and are alert and not terribly confused. Tomorrow and for a few days after, you'll need to stay with someone who can watch you when you sleep. You're going to have headaches, and if you have any nausea or vomiting, call your doctor, okay? No alcohol or drugs, no sports, no activities that require heavy concentration. Symptoms can last about a month or as little as a couple of days—including headaches, blurred vision, trouble sleeping, difficulty thinking, light and noise sensitivity, dizziness, and nausea. You can return to work when your symptoms go away. Check in with your doctor in a week, okay?"

I nod. After a few more minutes, the doctor leaves.

"He wants to fuck you."

I jerk my head toward the sound of Ricky's voice. "Pardon? Who, the doctor?"

He scoffs. "No, your boss. He wants you."

I roll my eyes. "Excuse me?

"I am a man, and a man knows. Stay away from him."

I laugh out loud. "Stay away from him?" I gasp, wiping my eyes. "Oh, that's amazing. I needed that. You are insane. He's a nice man. Calm down."

"Why would he come to see you like that? It's obvious, isn't it?"

"He's the reason I'm in here. I was taking his car. He's checking on me, probably doesn't want to get sued or fired. I'm supposed to go with him to a conference next week."

He nods, seeming to understand. "You could just be up front with him, you know. You two could just talk it all out instead of dancing around what has you both freaked out: him worried about you suing him for getting you into this mess, and you worried about getting fired for lying to him."

"Well, we could, but what fun is that?" I snort, laughing lightly. "So, you think you know everything then, huh?" I tease.

"I know what I know. And I'm not wrong."

I roll my eyes again. "So what? Who cares if you're right? You have no claim on me anymore."

I see the barb hit its mark. It's blatant, clouding his eyes and wiping the smirk off his face. For a moment, the briefest second, I'm sorry. Then I remember, and that falls away.

After a long, heavy silence, he sighs and says, "I told you she was never pregnant. She lied."

I open my mouth to snap at him, but he walks out the door. I know he'll be back, but I suddenly feel lighter now that the awkwardness has left the room right behind him.

# CHAPTER FIVE

## JUST WHEN I THOUGHT IT WAS OVER

IT'S LATE WHEN ALEX SHOWS UP. RICKY is still gone, and I'm lying half asleep when I hear the light, unsure knock and the "Yoo-hoo" through the crack in the door.

I sit up, smoothing covers, glancing up at the TV playing another rerun of *Friends* before I holler at her to come in. I texted her a couple hours ago, right after Ricky left. I needed a woman to talk to, someone to help me clear my head. Lily is the last person I would run to for advice that involves men, and being the recluse that I have been lately, I haven't made any new female friends. I've been too busy wallowing in my separation to even worry about it.

Alex walks in looking like she just left the gym in her Nike leggings and matching Dri-Fit rash guard in black and purple. A careful smile on her lips, she sets down a backpack and then is at my side. I smell her perfume, sweet and flowery.

"Hey, how are you? I'm sorry I'm here so late. I got hung up."

"It's fine. I'm sorry I didn't call you back."

She pats my hand; hers is cool. "The gym I go to is nearby, so it's nothing. Now, tell me what's going on. I'm your PO, but I can be a friend too if you need to chat."

I chew on my lip for a moment, fighting the cloud of the concussion and the drag of sleepiness as I try to clearly think about what I'm doing. Why I am telling her this? Because of the accident, the tests, the "just in case" and "what if" that now hang over me? I do need to tell someone, and as a woman, especially one who's older than I am, she'll get it. Hopefully she's a woman before she's a probation officer and I'm not shooting myself in the foot here. But she's always been nice, accommodating, not demanding like some POs are.

Then for a flash, I realize how pathetic I must look. No friends. No family. No confidants. Reaching out to call my probation officer because there just isn't anyone left to call.

"Can this be off the record? I don't want this to be anything official. I just kind of need someone to talk to, some advice, especially because of this accident."

She sits down, leaning in a bit. "Sure, sure. Of course. I'm always here for you."

People say that, but they don't really mean it. But here she is. Maybe she does mean it, who knows?

I take a deep breath and tell her what's going on. Everything that I know, which isn't much. I try to show her the needle mark, but it's hard to see now that I've had an IV in my arm. "I told the detective what I know, which isn't much. I don't expect anything to come from it, but then he said I have to have a rape kit done, and with my husband or ex-husband or whatever he is hovering…." I run the words together, verging on tears, overexcited and watching her look at me with concern on her face. My eyes burn, tears fighting to get out when I hold them back.

"Oh, Wren. Just because I'm a PO doesn't mean you have to be worried about coming to me with a problem. You can always talk to me, and I mean that. Why didn't you want to call the police?"

I sniff. "What can they really do? It's like reporting a bad dream or something. I only had to because the damn staff called them."

"I think you did the right thing. Even if nothing comes from it, maybe you'll at least get some peace."

"What if they think I'm lying?"

"Let your truth speak for itself and don't worry about that." She pauses a moment. "Can I see it?" she asks tentatively.

I glance down. "I guess." I pull my gown down a little, carefully lifting off the bandage, and she leans in, examining the mark.

"Oh, honey, that looks terribly painful. You really don't remember anything?"

I shake my head, covering the wound and myself back up. "Not a thing. If not for this, I would have no clue."

"He must want you to know he was there, then."

I swallow the words, it must be true. Funny how it never occurred to me. "Why?"

She shrugs. "Men are strange, dear. It's probably some twisted sexual deviation or something, right? Some like the fight, some don't." She shrugs as if she's talking about men who prefer redheads over brunettes. I suppose it's easy to be casual when it hasn't been you on the receiving end.

"What about the drugs he used? Will I get into trouble?"

She shakes her head. "No, not likely. Those type of drugs, GHB and all that sort, they aren't on regular tests. You have to ask for them. They aren't something people really use to get high. Do you want me to run the tests?"

I reach out and grab her arm. "No! No, please don't. Just leave it alone."

"But if you need to know later, it might help, right?"

I shake my head, panic rising in my throat like acrid bile. "No, no." All I can think about is someone twisting it around and me ending up in prison for six months or more. I'd rather deal with this alone, forever, than worry about that. "I would rather not. So, what should I do?"

"I think you've done all you can. Will you tell me if he comes back? You can come stay with me, or maybe we can put our heads together and come up with something. If you need to talk or anything, call me, okay? Day or night."

I watch her open her bag, grab a card, scribble down a number on it, and leave it on the side table. "This is my personal number. Call this one if you need me, okay?"

I nod.

"Promise me."

I smile. "I promise. I guess I do feel a little better after talking to you. I was so afraid to say any of this out loud."

She nods. "I'm sure. Makes it more real, I would guess. Maybe we can have dinner or something when you're feeling better."

"Okay. You won't get into trouble for hanging out with me?"

She laughs, waving her hand as if she's swatting the idea away like a bug in the air. "Hell no, that's silly. It's just a little DWI. You need to get some rest, but I'll check on you, okay? You don't be a stranger. I want to know what happens."

"I will, I promise. Go home. It's late."

In the end, after the door closes behind her and I've reached over to turn off my light, I'm glad I called her. Her reaction wasn't what I expected it to be. It would probably do me good to have a friend who's older, a woman, someone who's been there and done that and can tell me that I'm stupid when needed. A person with a head on her shoulders.

\*\*\*

The head injury makes me tired, but it's hard to sleep in this bed. I hear him, or someone, come into my hospital room early the next morning. Keeping my eyes pressed tight, I peek and see that it's Ricky, wearing dark-colored jeans and a sweater. I'm not sure why I don't want him to know I'm awake, but I keep silent until he walks back out, leaving only the phantom scent of strong, spicy cologne in his wake. Only then do I move, checking the time.

It's not even 6:00 a.m. yet. I wonder if he's been here all night and I just noticed. I fell asleep around eleven, and he wasn't here then. I think to look over at the chair; it's pulled out and looks slept in. He was here. He came back and slept here again. Must have left to think and shower, that kind of thing.

I turn on the TV and flip through crappy hospital cable until I find an acceptable nineties sitcom. So hard to focus, but I have to try. I'm supposed to leave Sunday for the conference, and I can't spare the overtime. Maybe getting away for a few days will put enough distance between me and whoever this is breaking into my house to deter him.

I've been struggling to concentrate on the TV for

almost an hour when my eyes get heavy. Just as I shut them, the door opens and in rolls someone with my breakfast. A big smile, a chipper "Good morning," and then they disappear again. I sit up, taking the top off to unveil the dish. Half a bagel, an omelet, fruit, and Canadian bacon. Not bad, I guess.

As I'm stuffing my face with mediocre eggs, Ricky walks in with a coffee in each hand. "Morning. Doc says you're going home today."

"Am I?"

"Yes. I'm going to take you."

"I have options. You don't have to." I push my food tray away, suddenly nauseated, and lean back carefully on the pillow, watching his face.

The nurse arrives with the medicine cart, logging in my meds and scanning my bracelet. She hands me a little cup with medicine in it, and I swallow the pills. Ricky sits on the edge of the bed and reaches for my hand. His is large and hot, wrapping around mine as if it's no big deal. As if he has no doubt as to what we are.

"I'm sure you do, but I'm taking you." He says it as if that's the end of the conversation.

I have plenty of people I can call for a ride, but no one I'd like to invite into my house to spend the night. Later, my phone starts to blow up.

**Oh, Wren, I heard what happened. Are you okay?**

**Can I help?**

**Do you need anything? I'll come**

get you.

**What did Doug say? Was he mad?**

My phone rings, and I see it's Alex from her personal number. I used to always feel a bit apprehensive talking to her when she called, but now it's easier after last night, like we broke the ice.

"Hi, Alex."

"Honey, how are you today? I got your results back. You're all clear."

I heave out a breath of relief. Thank God. I can't imagine actually going to prison for something that isn't even my fault. "Well, that's good." I force out a light laugh.

"How's your head?"

"Comes and goes. Doc said it'll be a few days. My boss was here yesterday. He wasn't mad, so far. I'm going home sometime today."

"Call me and I'll come and get you."

"I have a ride, thanks."

"Don't you need someone to sit with you at home for a night or two? Why don't you come stay with me until you're better? I have room. Don't think you have to be some kind of hero and do this alone."

"No, thank you, Alex. I'll be sure to take care of myself."

"You better. And keep me updated."

That evening Ricky keeps his word. Not knowing what to say, I let him help me into the wheelchair, trying not to notice how it feels to be so close to him. I feel tiny and feminine next to his bulk. As he pushes me out into the evening air, so many questions come into my mind. When he helps me into his Jeep and I wave him away when he tries to buckle me in, I wonder if I should have let him reach across me to catch his scent. I remember what it was like to lean in and put kisses on his neck. Then I wonder if she did it better, and the urge dies.

"Dinner?"

I'm so lost in my own thoughts as the wind whips through the open air of his Jeep that I almost don't hear him. Then my stomach rumbles and I turn to him. The movement makes me light-headed suddenly, and I close my eyes and grip my forehead to force the earth to stop spinning.

"Hey, you okay? You want to get something to eat?" He rests his firm hand on my thigh.

I uncover my face and blink away the dizziness. Nausea rolls through, but it's short term before the hunger returns.

The wind blows his hair; now I remember why his hair always looks so finger combed. His dark sunglasses hide his eyes and reflect my own pale, sickly face back at me when he looks my way. We drive, the sea on one side and the strip on the other.

"I'm sure I can find something to eat at home." I think on what I might have. Spoiled milk, peanut butter. Gross.

"I'll stop and get us something. We can eat here on

the beach."

I turn away so he won't see my smile. He's confusing to me, this bossy guy who's still somehow sweet and doting.

One drive-through later, we sit on the rocks watching the sun go down. I sit here and stuff lukewarm food into my mouth, food that I'm not really tasting because the close proximity of him has me all messed up inside. My head is hurting as I try to focus on the sounds of the ocean, the curling of waves on the shore, but it doesn't work. I cast my gaze out toward a ship on the horizon, wishing I was on it. He wants to try to be my hero, I know. This man thinks he can win me over by coming to my rescue, taking care of me.

I choke down the food and take a long drink of sweet tea before setting it back down on the rock beside me.

"You don't need to babysit me, Ricky," I finally say, breaking the silence.

He lets the words hang in the air for a moment, throwing me a sideways glance that I pretend not to notice.

"I'm not okay with leaving you alone and not knowing if your head is all right."

"I'm sure I'll be fine. Just drop me off at home. Let's go." I stop just short of saying, *I don't need you. I don't want you.* Somehow the words won't form, despite the quiet rage I feel inside; so instead, I stand up and gather my trash. I don't care if he follows me. I walk toward the car without another word, hoping my intent shows in my actions.

He does follow me, of course. The ride back to my apartment is silent and heavy with unspoken thoughts. When we arrive, Ricky shadows me from the management office at the apartment complex, where I collect my new keys, all the way to the door and then insists on coming inside, so I give in and let him. My head's in no condition for an argument. All I can do is hope he'll back off once he gets me settled in.

As we walk inside, my phone goes off with a text message alert from a number I don't know. I open it without thinking, then drop the phone and immediately bend over and vomit on the ceramic entryway after laying eyes on the message.

# CHAPTER SIX

## HEY THERE, SEXY

*I STRUGGLE AGAINST THE STRONG ARMS* that wrap around me after I heave my dinner all over the floor. Sobbing and blindly fighting against him, I look down at my phone as if it houses a demon. This isn't just some pervert in a club looking for a sick lay and getting off on scaring me. It's something worse, something bad. Really bad.

I start to shake and then finally give in to him because he's stronger than I am and won't let me go, despite my physical protest.

"Tell me what happened." The gentleness in his voice is gone. Now he's demanding, worried. The cop in him taking charge, I suppose. "Is it your head?"

"No, the text," I finally say, but even the word threatens to gag me. I retrieve my phone from the floor, use my fingerprint to unlock it, and hand it to him.

His face darkens, and I turn my head from the image after a moment. In it, I lay naked and obviously out cold, faceup on the bed. My bed, that night I went to the club, my blankets ripped off and in a mess half on the floor. My chest is emblazoned with that fucking bite mark, big as life. My panties are pulled down my thighs. No blood in this picture, just me and whoever is taking it. It's captioned like a Snapchat with a banner that reads "Hey there, Sexy."

"Is this from the other day?" His voice is heavy with quiet rage.

I shake my head. "No, it's from the first time."

He takes out his own phone and hits Dial while looking at me, seemingly calm, but his eyes tell me he's anything but.

"This has to be that night, because of the panties." I was lazy when I got dressed that night. Plain white granny panties, nothing cute. I didn't change into anything sexy, only meaning to have a few drinks with a friend and come back home a little buzzed.

When he hands the phone back to me, I suppose no one answered. Shocking. I watch him slide his phone in his rear left pocket. "Who are you trying to call?"

"You should have told me," he replies, ignoring my question.

"I didn't tell anyone. I wasn't even sure what happened."

He shakes his head, then pulls out his phone again, dialing once more. I rise to my feet, shaky, and tell him

I'm going to go get a towel.

"No, go sit down. I'll clean it up." His tone is forceful, so I sit down. My head hurts and my legs are trembling anyway.

"They're in the hall closet," I offer weakly. Again I wonder who he's calling as I watch him get paper towels and bleach to clean up the mess. He dries it up with a bath towel while chatting with someone, but I don't listen, I can't. All I hear is my own voice in my head, screaming at me. Blood rushing in my ears, my heart pounding too hard and fast.

"You can't stay here."

I push past the din of my own anxiety to try to hear what he's saying.

"I have to. This is my home."

"I won't let you." His stare is a dare, I can see it. Daring me to challenge him, to force me to listen.

"Why can't I stay here?"

"He'll come back. You're coming home with me."

*Come back.*

*He'll come back.*

The words pound out a rhythm in my mind that I don't appreciate. One I can't accept.

No one is after me. They can't be.

"Who did you call? And how do you know he'll come back? Maybe he's just getting off on fucking with me."

He crosses thick arms over an even thicker chest. "You're still my wife. I love you. I won't let you get yourself killed because you're pissed off at me." He disappears down the hall, and I follow.

He loves me. That's a laugh.

I walk into my bedroom. He's got my pink Nike duffel bag and is packing clothes for me. "What are you doing?"

"Packing your stuff. After the cops come, we're going home."

I want to cry. Home. I knew he still lived in our house. Of course he would. But I never imagined myself there again. To be quite honest, it sounds lovely. Then his other words hit my brain and I frown.

"You called a cop? You had no right. How dare you presume—"

He cuts me off, bending at the waist and grabbing my face in his gentle hand. "I had every right, because I know what this is. He's toying with you. He'll kill you when he's finished."

Kill me.

I didn't just hear that.

But I did.

He said this person wants to kill me. How could he know that?

I feel the blood drain away from my face, and the screaming in my head starts again. I can't think about what he just told me, can't let it sink in. Maybe if I don't, he'll be wrong, or crazy, or whatever. Anything to make it not true.

But it gets through anyway, taking root in my brain

until I can't think of anything else.

There is a big difference between what we want and what we need. What I want is to run out the door and pretend I didn't hear it. But I *need* to know. Common sense forces me to ask the very question that terrifies me the most.

"How do you know?" I finally whisper, choking on tears. "You aren't a cop anymore."

"Because I know. He will kill you."

Kill? As in dead? Murdered? A sob breaks from my lips, despite how I try to hold it in. "What? How…? I…," I stammer, not sure of what to say.

He lets go of me before rising to his full height. "I'll tell you later. We have to get out of here. Grab what you need."

Quickly, I assist him in packing, tossing in the few things I need, imagining I'll be coming home in a few days. That or headed off with Doug to the conference, and by the time I get back, all will be forgotten.

He tells me that the police will come to our house, not this apartment. I don't answer; I have no words. I can't even process what is happening. I feel like I'm standing here outside my body as I cram stuff almost blindly into the duffel bag.

I climb back into the Jeep. The ride is silent; though I have so many questions, I don't know where to start, and I wonder if I really want answers. Maybe I'd rather stay in denial, pretend nothing is wrong.

Ricky turns onto the road that runs alongside the

coast. The seawall. The sun, now an orange ball of fire, dips slowly into the ocean. It's gloriously peaceful to see, but it does nothing for the chaos inside me. He pulls his Jeep in front of an ocean-view townhouse on stilts. I'm assisted up the steps and into the door, where a golden retriever greets us, sniffing my feet and wiggling his butt as if he's terribly excited to see me.

I can't help but smile. My dog. My home. "Hey, Duke!" I crouch and hug him, the terribly excited dog licking all over my face.

"You want anything?"

"No, thanks." I hesitate for a moment. "Ricky, what happens now?"

He stops moving around and sits down beside me. "You have to talk to the police. They need to go to your apartment. And you need a new phone number. Someone is after you."

"Why me?"

He shrugs. "I don't know."

I watch his face, my heart beating in my ears as I wait for the answer. "He's killed others?"

"Yes. Six in two years. He toys with them before he kills them. It's not over, Wren."

Our eyes meet, his gray searching my brown.

I finally scoff. "This is ridiculous. It has to be a mistake. I'm nothing special. I don't draw that kind of attention. Come on. It's got to be a copycat or something. How do you know this is what you think this is?"

"I just know. Trust me. I'd never mess around with your life."

*Liar. You did mess around with my life when you did what you did.*

I blink, looking away from the depth of the intensity coming from his eyes. "I want to know."

He sighs heavily and looks down at the floor. "I'll tell you another time. It's too much for one day, especially with your head the way it is. I'm going to tuck you in, and then I'm going to go for a jog."

"I'll be fine right here." I pat the couch.

"You can take the bed, Wren."

"I'm fine. Really. I just want to watch TV." To try and forget. To pretend.

He eyes me as he stands, seeming uncertain. "You promise?"

I nod. "Promise."

"Okay then."

I'm tucked onto the couch with pillows and a big fuzzy blanket, my favorite one, worn thin in spots. He hands me the remote and a Yeti cup full of ice water. After making me swear to call him for anything at all, he and the dog head out for a night run.

It isn't long before I start to get sleepy.

\*\*\*

It's dark. A deep voice calls my name, and I blink the confusion away and struggle to remember. Am I still in the hospital?

I squint, taking in my surroundings. Looks homier. The bed is comfier.

That's right, I'm back home. It's Ricky waking me up to check on me.

"Hey, it's me. Do you know where you are?"

I sit up, wincing because my head hurts. The memory comes back, fighting through the headache and the drowsiness. "I'm home. I fell asleep?"

"Yeah. I didn't wake you up because you need the rest. You okay? Confused? How's your head feel?"

I look up into his eyes and sigh. I realize he's sitting here with no shirt on. He's covered in muscle and tattoos, but it's too dark to make them out. It's a struggle, but I pull my gaze off his body and back to his face. I miss him, and I hate it. "I'm okay. I know what's going on and where I am."

His hair is tousled from sleep, but he still looks tired. "What time is it?" I mutter around a yawn.

"Little after midnight."

Being so close to him, in this house, in the middle of the night swells something in my chest. It would be so easy to reach out and touch him, feel his hot skin under my hand. I'm not sure if I should, so I don't.

"Thanks for checking on me." My voice is small.

He smiles. "It's no problem. You want something for your head?"

I have no idea. I tell him as much with a shrug, and he gets up with a nod, headed for my pill bottles on the counter.

"I've got so much to do tomorrow," I mumble to no one.

"You need to rest your brain. Don't overdo it."

I swallow the pills with a mouthful of water and set the Yeti back where it was before lying back down.

"You can come sleep in the bed if you want to," he says quietly, standing up.

My brain spins at the offer. *Bad idea. Bad, bad idea.* But it would be comforting, easy. It doesn't have to mean anything. "You mean with you?"

He shrugs. "Sure, or if you want, I'll sleep in here. But I mean, considering… it's not a stretch to share."

I feel myself flush and am grateful that it's dark and he likely can't see. "I don't know."

"You need a good night's sleep. And frankly, I'm so tired that I'll sleep way better with you beside me. I miss you." To my surprise, he leans down and kisses my forehead. "Please. I promise I won't try anything."

I feel tears burning in my throat. I nod, too tired to care or fight.

In bed, I'm instantly home. Comforted. The heat from his body warms me, even though he isn't touching me. He rolls away, his back to me, and I feel tears roll off my face to the pillow. Comforting, yet it still really hurts. The bed that was once mine. Even as I sink into the familiarity of it, I wonder who he might've had in this bed in the last few months. If *she* was ever here with him. The thought makes me hate him, but the bed makes me love him. I turn my back to him, closing my eyes to the reality of it all.

"Night, Wren."

"Night, Ricky." There's no tremble in my voice, thankfully. I fall asleep thinking about how much I miss him, how much I want my life back, and how much I hate him for taking it away from me. This isn't home anymore and won't ever be again.

Selfish bastard.

\* \* \*

The next morning, I wake up in his arms. He's still asleep, and I'm curled into his chest. His smell is relaxing, and I feel sleepy again.

I realize then that the police didn't come, and I'm confused. He called them, so why didn't they come?

Deciding to get out of bed before he wakes up and sees me in his arms, I rise, change, and then go make coffee. I feed Duke before letting him into the backyard, fill a cup with coffee, and then settle onto the couch.

"Morning." He yawns, coming into the room in just pajama pants. "You hungry?"

"A little. Why didn't the police come last night?"

He runs his hand through his hair, only succeeding in making it crazier than it was. "I called the detective and told him we would meet him today."

"Why didn't you tell me that? You acted like they were coming here."

He looks at me for a moment, the blank stare

answering my question. He did it to make sure I came with him without a fight, knowing I would stay if he got me here. I just shake my head, not knowing how to respond, not feeling like arguing.

He walks off, moving in the kitchen. He's going to cook.

Flashes of that picture keep popping into my head at odd times. I turn on the TV and try to push back all the emotions, the confusion and the fear.

I don't say anything except a muttered "thanks" when he brings me a plate—mushroom, sausage, and cheese omelet with toast. He passes me a bottle of my favorite hot sauce and then walks away, a sulking look on his face. He knows he was wrong.

I eat in silence, then go shower and change.

# CHAPTER SEVEN

## NUMBER SEVEN

AFTER THE SHOWER, I pull on JEANS and a sweatshirt, then sit on the bed with my phone and check in with a few people. I text Doug and tell him how I'm doing, then text Alex, letting her know that I have to go see the police today and I'm staying with Ricky, just for now.

I call Lily, and we talk for a bit. I don't tell her about the stranger stalking me or that the police are involved, just the accident, the conference, Ricky, and how I can't stay alone due to the doctor's orders—generic, harmless stuff. I don't know why I can't let myself open up to Lily, but I just can't. Lily is my age, but she's nothing like me. She loves men and assumes that all women must love them the way she does. I wouldn't go as far as to label her or call her a name like "slut," because no one can know what makes a person the way they are or what their true motivations are, but she does sleep around. More than once, I've gone out with her and lost her to a guy she's met, getting a text saying she's going home with him. That's why when we ever do go anywhere, I don't depend on her for transport anymore. She's mostly just company for me during a lonely patch in my life.

She giggles, drops jokes about Doug and me being in a hotel out of town, that sort of thing. I joke with her, laughing, going along with it. I don't want to make her feel bad for it with the truth.

When we hang up, I finish my hair by blow-drying it out upside down, which makes my head throb. I crunch up my long curls with curling product, leaving it half dry to prevent frizzing.

I walk out into the living room and find Ricky completely clothed, shoes on, the works. He must have dressed while I was in the shower. He's cleaned the kitchen too, plus folded up my blankets on the couch.

"You ready?"

I blink at him. "Ready? You expect to come with me?"

"Yes."

I shake my head. "I can manage. I'll call an Uber."

"Why not drive?"

I swallow thickly and take a deep breath. *I guess the truth will come out eventually.* "I lost my license for a while. I'm on probation for DWI. The weekend what's-her-face showed up, after I left I went and got drunk. Then I got arrested. Don't even think about giving me any shit. Blame yourself. Blame her. I know you know, Ricky." There's no way he can't. Pretending stupidity is worse; it tells me that he cares only when it's convenient for him. "Just stop playing dumb."

I turn my back, heading for my purse.

"Wren—"

"Leave it alone. Just forget it," I mutter, grabbing my bag while pulling up the Uber app on my phone. "I'll handle it myself."

"You have no idea what you're in the middle of. It's not safe. You can't get into the car with some stranger not knowing who's after you." No confession. No "I'm sorry, I should have said something. Should have helped you back then when it all happened." Nothing. No acknowledgment whatsoever. I huff, shaking my head at his *you need me* bullshit.

"Watch me."

"Please don't." His eyes are worried, wider. "Let me come with you."

"Why?"

He swallows, running a frustrated hand over his face. "Her... that woman, her name was Angela. She was nuts I think, at least a little. She lied about being pregnant. It was... well...." He takes a deep breath. "She died about two months ago... murdered. She was calling me, telling me that someone was after her, breaking in. I thought she was just trying to get my sympathy, get to me. She sent me pictures of bites just like yours. She was killed by a serial killer who's killed six women—including Angela. I had no idea this killer existed until after her death. I was the patrol officer who was first on scene. I caught the initial call, but of course I didn't know it was her until I got there."

It's the first time I've ever heard him use her name, but my brain fast-forwards past that part. "What? She's dead?" Should I feel happy? Sad? Twirl around in circles and laugh and tell him she got what she deserved for stealing him away?

I guess that would be a bit much.

I stand with my mouth partially open, but no words come out. He twirls his keys again, and I fall into the worn suede recliner behind me. "So, he's really a serial killer? What is the bite, like a calling card?"

He blows out a breath and runs his hands through his hair. "As far as the bite, no one knows. Yes, he's a serial killer. The problem is, the police have no living victims that they know of. The reports before the fact are spotty. Some women don't say a thing until it's too late. They find all this shit on their phones and stuff." He fades out as if he doesn't know what to say.

"I haven't seen anything on the news. How do you know all this?"

"Because the chief of police is a moron and won't do a press release. I've told you how he is." He shrugs.

I swallow, but my mouth is dry. "Who is this guy?"

He shifts his weight. "They tagged him as the SMS Killer. He taunts his victims via text message and social media. They're guessing that he plays with them for some weeks before he kills them, going by the evidence on their phones. Not what you'd call typical."

"No, I suppose not, if there is such a thing as normal for a murderer," I mutter, though not really to him, more to the air around me, I suppose. The name echoes in my head, the image of the picture I got bouncing around right along with it.

Serial killer. This isn't real life. Surely I'm the victim of some elaborate reality show hoax or something.

But then that truth screams at me from somewhere in the back of my mind. No one ever thinks it'll happen to them. It's always someone else. Some nameless stranger, a pretty face that's posted online or on the news. A viral post with thousands of condolence comments from strangers. Not me.

But it is me. This time I'm the pretty, smiling face on the news.

Number seven.

Death. The end.

No, this isn't it for me. Dying at twenty-six with half a husband, no kids. Just random friends to come mourn for me until someone else takes my place at my desk and I'm a story they tell people on Halloween.

Fuck. I can't breathe.

My chest feels tight, and tears start to stream from my eyes as I struggle to take a deep breath, fighting against lungs that don't want to cooperate. My vision blurs as that light-headed feeling returns. I gasp, suddenly trembling. "Oh God. I don't want to die.

I'm not ready."

"Hey, hey, you're okay. Breathe slowly." Ricky drops to his knees in front of me, taking my now wet face into his hands, staring into my eyes in some attempt to calm me.

"I can't breathe right." My voice chokes off on a sob. I wince, my chest tight and painful. "My chest hurts."

"I know. You're going to give yourself a panic attack. Slowly, breathe in as I count." He counts to ten, again and again. I'm supposed to breathe in and out on his word, so I do, and it helps. I can feel my lungs again; my vision starts to clear. But I'm still shaking, crying.

"I don't want to die." I whimper, my lip trembling like a frightened child's would. "What do I do?"

"We talk to Detective Small today. That's a start. Then we'll go from there. One step at a time. I'll do everything I can to keep you safe."

Safe. Like he kept her safe? Angela?

"I think your ride just pulled up. Do you really want to do that? Get in the car with a stranger?"

I look out one of his big picture windows and see a plain silver Toyota with a bald, middle-aged male driver. Fear settles over me like a blanket, heavy and suffocating. I can't get a deep breath, like someone is squeezing my lungs and they won't fully inflate.

The killer could be anyone. It could be Ricky, for all I know. But no, that can't be. If he wanted to do something to me, he would have last night.

I back up. "Yeah, I guess you have a point there." Got to be realistic. Can't let it make me crazy just yet. I have weeks for that, apparently.

"Come on, I'll take you."

I agree just as I cancel the car from the app on my phone. We don't leave until the guy has driven away, though I still feel nauseated when I follow Ricky out the door.

# CHAPTER EIGHT

## YOU CAN'T HANDLE THE TRUTH

BY THE TIME WE REACH THE POLICE department, my nausea is gone and I can breathe again. I debate on throwing a temper tantrum, thinking he has no right to force me into this. But then I remember those two not-so-little words and I stop cold.

Serial killer.

I want to know more, but I'm not sure how to approach it. What are the odds that Ricky would know the last victim as well as me? How strange. It's not like she looked like me. I'm a size twelve; she was a two at most. I'm blonde with curly hair; she had long dark hair. She was younger than me, so whatever profile this killer has must not be about looks. She and I don't fit. I understand now why Ricky didn't tell me, why he stayed with me in the hospital and hasn't left my side.

Following him inside in a daze, I sit in an old chair in the lobby that's upholstered in what I suppose used to be red leather-like fabric but is now worn pink and cracked with overuse. I stare off into nothing until a door opens and Detective Small calls my name.

I stand up and turn to Ricky. He's not getting up.

"Aren't you coming with me?" I hear the panic in my voice that makes it an octave higher. I didn't imagine going through this alone. Not now that I know what this really is. How is he not following me?

He looks up from his phone, then sets it in his lap.

"I thought it would be too personal to talk about in front of me. I don't want to—"

"You haven't seemed to mind that for the last two days. You're playing the understanding guy now?" I glance over at Detective Small, who's waiting without a word in an olive-colored shirt tucked into dark pants, a loose tie under his collar. "Just get up. Come with me. I can't do this alone." I pause, then add, "Please." I don't care about being stubborn right now. The fight has gone right out of me, despite my best efforts. I just can't sit in there and feel like I'm being interrogated for my own stupidity all alone.

"Are you sure?"

Our eyes meet. "Yes, I am."

I'm really not. Not at all. I'm just scared shitless.

I feel like I can breathe again when he finally gets up, following me though the door.

Led down what seems a maze of halls and through a few doors, we finally settle in a small office. Detective Small sits down and glances between us before speaking.

"I'm not sure what you've been told, but I'd like to just start at the beginning and work from there." He sets out a recorder and turns it on. "I'll be recording this to add to the case file. In the room are myself, Detective Small, and Enrique and Wren Addison." He rattles off the date and time, then leans way back in a chair that squeaks under his girth. "Mrs. Addison, tell me about what happened."

I tell him about the text and show him the picture on my phone. I watch nervously as he takes reading glasses out and puts them on, looking down his nose at the image with serious eyes. He asks me to forward the picture to an email, which I do.

"Have you had any strange phone calls or texts other than this?" he asks.

"No. Ricky told me about the killer, about Angela." Her name tastes bad in my mouth.

Small ends the recording and then shuts it off. He glances between us, then leans back heavily. "What do you think about what he told you?" He sticks a piece of gum into his mouth and offers us some. We both decline. I actually want some, but it'll only make me thirsty.

"I don't know. He told me about Angela, that she died. That you guys don't know much, but he wouldn't go into detail. Is this really a serial killer? Is there a profile? Why me?"

"We haven't figured out how he finds his victims.

That's usually one of the last pieces of the puzzle, I'm afraid. He's right, I would say that you're likely the next on his radar. Mrs. Addison, you are in danger. Can you leave town? Or—"

I hold up a hand. "I won't just stop my life; I can't do that. I'm on probation. I have limitations."

He nods. "Of course. I'm still waiting on the results of your rape kit. Shouldn't be but a few more days." That's a lie and I know it. The forensic lab takes months to get anything back. They did a whole story on it last month on the news, talking about how backed up they are and how it's delaying cases right and left. I don't call him out; there's no point in it. Hopefully they pushed this one to the front of the line, and if they didn't, maybe they will now. Before I die rather than after.

I look up at Ricky, who has his eyes cast down. He looks lost in thought.

"We need to get the CSU team over to your apartment, have them look around." The detective's voice pulls my eyes off my sullen husband. I wonder if he's thinking of her.

I furrow my brow, frowning. "What's that mean?" You would think I'd know more being married to a cop, but he never talked about work. He used to tell me that he left all that at the door when he walked out for the day and wouldn't burden me with the darkness of it. It always bothered me that he refused to share such a huge part of his life, but on the other hand, I understood. I know some things just can't be discussed, so I would let it go rather than allow myself to turn into an annoying nag of a wife. So here I sit like any other citizen, clueless when I should know so much more about the inner workings of a police department.

"Means we need to get a crime scene unit over to your apartment to see if there might be any evidence left behind that you missed. Blood is almost impossible to get rid of altogether, so there's sure to be something, somewhere."

"You can be there if you like," Ricky adds.

"Will you take anything?" I ask Small. "From my apartment, I mean."

"Only if it's physical evidence. Say, if we find blood on your sheets, we would take them. But we would inventory everything."

Do I really want to sit by and watch them tear up my house? No, I don't think I do. "I think I'd rather pass on hanging around. Can you just take my key? I'll get it from you later."

He nods. "Of course. I'll get it to you this evening or tomorrow morning. Be careful, Mrs. Addison. I'll spare you the lecture, but no amount of police work is going to protect someone if they aren't careful."

"Thanks, I appreciate that. Just kind of hard to be on the lookout when you don't know what you're watching for." I sigh, standing up.

"I understand. Keep my card. Call me day or night."

I hand over my house key, hoping I'm not making

a mistake, but I remember that my life and the life of any other woman is more important than me protecting my stuff from being taken by the police. I know they'll make a mess, but I'll deal with it. I'd rather be alive to clean it up than be dead with a neat house.

It's all so surreal. I'm not old enough to be thinking about the end of my life. But then that one question begs to be answered: If you knew you were going to die, what would you do?

*Am I going to die?*

# CHAPTER NINE

## DINNER'S AT SIX

HE'S KILLED SIX WOMEN. HAVE ANY others survived? Will I be the first? Or is this it for me? I bet they all thought they would be the one who lived. Every last one of them. Now here I am, destined to be a chapter in a true crime novel someday. Victim of a killer that will probably end up as a made-for-TV movie and a Halloween costume someday.

There's so much I haven't done, so much I've never thought about. I haven't even thought of kids yet. I'm too broke to go on some end-of-life spree and go crazy traveling or shopping or jumping out of airplanes or whatever people might do. Ricky makes decent money teaching now, but I can't depend on him anymore. I left him. I can't go back.

By the time I come back to reality, we're on the highway. The wind is in my hair, whipping through the open top of Ricky's Jeep as we drive. He reaches over and takes my hand, then brings it to his lips for a kiss. "Wren, talk to me."

I pull my hand away and wipe it on my pants. "Just thinking about my bucket list."

"Don't. You won't die."

"You can't know that. Don't worry, I don't really have one."

He makes a noise that sounds like a grunt. "I do know. You'll be fine. You have to be. They'll catch this guy."

"I think you have some things you need to share. You aren't telling me everything."

He nods. "You're right, I'm not. But with your head the way it is, maybe being overwhelmed with the truth is a bad idea."

"I'm not some delicate flower, you know."

"I know. But this is different."

He parks in the lot of a seafood restaurant on the seawall, and I get out without argument. I'm starving.

After we're seated, I'm stirring sugar into my tea when my phone rings.

"Hi, Mr. Larson," I answer.

"Wren, honey, how are you?"

"I'm managing. My head seems a bit better today."

"Good. Hey, are we still on for the conference Monday? It won't be too hard on you, I promise. I just need someone there to help me with my email and stuff while I'm busy. I also need you during sessions because I'm a presenter."

I chew on my lip for a minute. "What if I get there and it's too much for me? I'd hate to—"

"Wren, we'll work it out, whatever happens. I promise. I'd like to meet you for dinner tomorrow to discuss the details. Can I pick you up at six?"

I take a drink of tea, trying to process this as fast as my damaged head will allow. What will Ricky say? What *can* he say? He and I aren't back together, and this is work. It's not anything else.

But he'd tell me I'd be wrong to travel, that I need to heal. I'm sure I do, but I also think getting away for a few days might help.

"Okay, I guess we can do that."

"Good. I'll get back to you with the address. We'll have fun, I promise."

"Okay, thanks."

When I hang up, Ricky is watching me without a smile. "You're going, aren't you?"

I set my phone on the table and pick up my menu for something to hide behind. "I need the money, and maybe if I get away, he'll forget me or something. Maybe it's not this SMS guy, you know. It could be someone else."

"You need to heal. I'll give you money."

"I'll be okay. He won't overwork me. And keep your money."

He takes a roll from the bread basket and proceeds to violently butter it. I raise an eyebrow at the possessive display and almost smile.

"I don't like this."

"I can tell." I smirk.

Our eyes meet across the table. "Look." He sighs, bread in hand. "I want you to come home. You don't have to forgive me or anything, but it's not safe for you to be alone. At least if you're home, I can protect you."

I butter a roll and take a bite before I answer him. This seems to bring a smile back to his face, and he finally starts to eat.

"Before I leave, I want you to tell me everything." It's not an answer to his proposal, but he knows that what he says to me now will determine my reaction later.

Silence falls between us for a moment. He agrees just as the waiter shows up.

\* \* \*

I leave tomorrow morning and still haven't been able to sit down with Ricky to talk to him. I returned to my apartment to pack, then came back home hoping he might spark a conversation, but he has yet to do it. I'm starting to really wonder if what he knows is just so bad that he's afraid to tell me, and now I'm almost scared to ask him.

He's sitting on the couch reading a Stephen King book as I get ready for my dinner with Doug. When I went back to my apartment today, I almost cried when I saw the mess the police left behind. But I stepped over it and managed to gather what I needed for the trip, leaving the chaos behind a locked door when I left. I tried not to look, tried to see past it, determined to deal with it later. I've left it locked securely behind a matching door in the back of my mind.

Now my bags are ready, sitting by the front door. I'm wearing a pantsuit that I usually wear to work and am probably sweating through the silk blouse as I pace, a little freaked out over this dinner.

Doug arrives, knocking on the door. I glance at Ricky, who doesn't budge except to peer over the top of his paperback. I find my boss in jeans and a polo shirt behind the door, smiling. I've never seen him dressed in anything other than a suit, and casual looks good on him.

I grab my purse and legal pad holder, pausing to think for a moment about my goodbye to Ricky. "I'll be back soon." I smile.

Ricky stands up, book in hand, and I'm surprised when he gives me a soft kiss on the mouth. He grins at me when I pull back. "Okay, baby." He kisses me again, and I turn and walk out the door. I know he was marking his territory, and I guess I half expected it. I suppose it's understandable, but it irks me that he thinks he has the right to lay any sort of claim after what he did. It's not about me really, just that he doesn't want someone else to have me. It's about losing what he thinks should be his. Asshole.

"How is your car after the accident?" I ask, getting into a luxury rental SUV.

"The insurance company is going to total it, I'm afraid."

"Oh, crap. Mr. Larson, I'm so sorry about that—"

"Wren, call me Doug. And it's not your fault. The police faulted the other driver. You're not responsible."

"Even so…." I sigh. Does he know that I didn't even have a valid license? About my DWI? I chew on my lip, struggling to appear calm and relaxed when I'm anything but. "Mr.—I mean Doug, is it true that you got into trouble? Lily mentioned it to me."

I don't know why I asked. I regret it almost the second it comes out of my mouth. Probably just another office rumor gone wild.

He pulls into the parking lot of an Italian place and turns to me after shutting off the engine, his blue eyes studying me. "I did, but that's my own stupid fault. I shouldn't have had you running personal errands. That isn't what you're paid for. The company won't pay your bills, so I am."

*Should I tell him thank you? I'm sorry? I should have said no?* I swallow thickly. "I don't know what to even say," I finally blurt, feeling like an idiot for not being more eloquent.

He smiles at me. "You don't have to say anything. Let's go inside." He grabs his briefcase from the back seat, and I follow him in.

He orders lobster, wine, fancy hors d'oeuvres—the works. I'm stuffed to the gills on a meal that cost an easy two or three hundred bucks, sipping wine and wondering if that's okay with my concussion. It's so crisp and sweet and smooth, I can't stop myself. He smiles and fills my glass again, and I tell myself I need to drink slowly or he'll likely just keep refilling it for me.

"Okay, so let's get down to business," he says, pulling an envelope out of his briefcase. "This is your plane ticket and your hotel reservation. I have a company laptop for you that I will bring with me. Plane leaves for San Francisco at seven o'clock tomorrow morning. We'll get there around eleven maybe. The first day of the conference is mostly just checking in and orientation, and there's a welcome thing that evening. None of that even starts until four, so we can hang out until then. The next day they have breakfast, different programs and presenters. There's a dinner that night. Wednesday is the same, ends a little after lunch. I couldn't get a flight back that night, so we head back Thursday around lunchtime. The reason I need you is that I'm presenting. I need you to help me out, get me ready, do what I need during the session, things like that."

I blink, trying to absorb what he just told me through the brain fog and the wine. How am I supposed to remember this schedule?

I open my legal pad and put my pen to paper, but he stops me, hand on mine. "Sweetie, don't worry. There will be a welcome packet, and the schedule will be inside. Don't memorize it now. Just be at the airport in the morning."

I nod; what else can I do? Closing my legal pad, I set it aside and take the envelope. Lots of downtime, it sounds like. Time that he might want to hang out, chat. But then again, maybe he'll hook up with some of his lawyer friends and I can just chill in the hotel. Might not be so bad. Paid to do squat.

"We're going to have a great time." He smiles, leaning back, tilting his head. "Don't you think so?"

"Yeah, I'm sure it'll be awesome." I finish my wine.

We finish our dinner, and I manage to make it back to Ricky's without incident. Nothing inappropriate happens. It's close to nine when I walk in the door, set my stuff down, shed my shoes and jacket, and plop down beside him on the couch.

"How did it go?"

"Painless. Nice dinner. He told me the plane leaves at seven in the morning for San Francisco. Be back Thursday afternoon."

He nods, then rests his head on the back of the couch with his eyes on me. "How do you feel about it?"

"I don't even know. I guess I will soon enough."

Our eyes meet in the dim light, and I wonder if he's planning to keep his promise. The one he made to tell me all the things that he's been keeping secret. I've almost been able to forget it all over the last few hours with the anticipation and mild freak-out I've been having over this Doug thing, but here it is again. The center of everything.

"You want some coffee or something?"

I shake my head. "No, thanks."

"Wren, are you sure you're ready to hear everything I know?"

I nod, but inside is a little voice that's screaming at me to say no so I can keep pretending nothing is wrong. If I keep pretending hard enough, maybe it'll become the truth, a new reality generated by the power of positive thinking.

"I'm ready."

Yeah, right.

He sits up and takes a deep breath.

# CHAPTER TEN
## I TOLD YOU SO

*RICKY*
*FOUR MONTHS AGO*

*I WATCHED, STUNNED, AS WREN PACKED* a bag and walked out, tears on her face. She screamed, she yelled, she threw our wedding picture at me, succeeding in smashing the flat-screen TV when I ducked and it hit the screen instead. She asked questions and then refused to listen to the answers, not allowing me to explain, to apologize, to beg.

I tried, I really did. Nothing worked.

Then she was gone.

Angela is fucking crazy. She worked at the police department back in records. She sat in the back at a little desk, sorting police reports and sending stuff off to the DA's office, handling public records requests. I'd go in there too often. I knew I was playing a dangerous game; I don't know why I did it. One day she asked me for a ride home. I should have told her no, but I couldn't do it.

Yes, I did sleep with her, only once. I was stupid and horny, and she was more than willing. Easy. Irresistible, and she knew just what she was doing. Before I knew it, she was climbing into my lap, lifting a sundress to show me that she didn't have on any panties, asking me if I wanted some. She felt me harden and smiled, then pulled my hand between her legs and unbuttoned my jeans. Before I could realize what I was doing, she was groaning and I was balls deep right there in her driveway.

I felt like shit when it was over. She dragged me inside, gave me a beer, teased me a little about work. She was no stranger to me; I saw her every day. She asked me to stay the night, but I declined. I kissed her goodnight, and I went home. I never touched her again.

I had trouble sleeping for a while after that. Angela tried to get with me for months after it happened. She texted me so much I had to block her number. I was verging on going to my boss to complain about her, but making complaints like that in a police department just isn't the same as going to HR in the private sector. I ultimately told her point-blank to leave me alone, that it was a mistake. She teared up and told me she loved me. I felt sick.

It was a week after that conversation that I came home and found her standing on my porch, talking to my wife. I knew it was too late. What I didn't know was the lengths she would go to thinking she could win me. Telling Wren that she was pregnant when I knew it wasn't possible was like a nightmare. Our one-night stand had happened months before, whereas the harassment went on for ages before it all came to a head. But Wren wouldn't believe me, wouldn't listen. I guess I can't blame her there. If the shoe were on the other foot... I can't even think about what I would have done.

I tried to tell Wren, but she wouldn't believe me. I had to drag Angela to her car to get her to leave, and she tried to kiss me. That was when Wren stopped listening. When she turned away and I knew I might have lost her for good.

After Wren left, I tried to keep busy. Angela kept following me around, and I thought about leaving the department, but I refused to let her run me off. Angela would call and text me, getting around being blocked by calling from different numbers.

She showed up crying in the middle of the night at one point, telling me that someone had drugged and sexually assaulted her. She opened her shirt and showed me this nasty bite on her chest. She had on no bra, of course. I assumed that she was nuts and making shit up to get into my life.

It went on for weeks. Then maybe about six weeks ago, I got a call on the radio. I was oblivious when it came through. Dead on scene, called in by hotel staff.

I took the call, turned around, and was en route.

I flashed my badge to a wide-eyed, pale woman behind a desk. She nodded and handed me a room key. "It's room 4506 on the fourth floor." She didn't offer to have me escorted, so I thanked her and headed for the bank of elevators off to the left of the lobby.

When I stepped off the elevator, the hallway was quiet. Not a peep. Having been an officer for a few years now, I was no stranger to death. I steeled myself, having no real details of what was behind this door. All dispatch could tell me was a very distraught woman had called and said a guest had died. The caller wouldn't or couldn't give any more detail.

I whistled as I walked down the hall. Palming the doorknob, I inserted the key and threw the door open.

At first, I couldn't focus. Unable to make out just what I was seeing as I moved into the doorway, I was careful not to cross the line without the proper precautions. The first thing I saw was a plain room with an ugly peach bedspread colored red, as if a paint bomb had gone off. The bed was soaked, the walls splattered, the ceiling as well. A few personal belongings were lying here and there—her purse, her shoes, her phone. Clothes were tossed over the back of a chair; the TV was off. I looked around, struggling to see anything but her, but in the end I couldn't not look.

She was somehow still lovely, even in death. Even with the blueish-gray, waxy skin and the vacant eyes, she had a pretty face. Long dark hair soaked and matted.

Body sliced and riddled with stab wounds, cuts, open throat, open wrists. Seemingly drained of blood, she had no chance.

It was Angela. Dead. Obviously dead. No reason to go in and check for a pulse; the gaping throat wound and buckets of blood told me what I needed to know.

The edges of my vision dimmed as my mind's eye flashed to her riding me, whimpering. All the interaction after, the calls for help that I didn't believe. I ignored her. If I had listened, she might not have been fileted in that bed. I stepped back into the hallway, grabbed for my radio with shaking hands, then thought to reach forward and close the door.

"Seven-Adam-Fourteen to dispatch."

"Go ahead."

"I need CSU and the on-call detective to this scene. Go ahead and get the medical examiner as well. Unnatural causes."

"Clear."

I slid down the wall with my head in my hands.

All I could do was sit and guard the door in the time I waited for backup to arrive. Eventually I got to my feet, not wanting to appear shaken when they arrived. I was pacing when Detective Small lumbered off the elevator. His eyes met mine wearily, as if he knew what he was walking into. The man's been doing this for over twenty years, he's no fool.

I met him halfway.

"What is it?" he asked.

"Homicide. Bloodbath. Her throat was slit."

He sighed heavily. "Damn. Did you go in?"

"No, she's obviously been dead for some hours. I didn't pass the threshold." I paused and cleared my throat. "Hey, I do need to talk to you though." My voice was smaller than I intended.

"Why?"

"I know—knew—her. You did too. I mean...." I floundered, reaching for words. "It's Angela from records. I didn't want to say anything over the radio."

His eyes rounded slightly, obviously surprised. "Damn, are you sure?"

I nodded. "Yes, I'm sure." Of course I was. I should have told him, I knew I should, but I couldn't make my mouth say the words that we had a short fling. It just wouldn't come out of my mouth. He knew my marriage broke up, but I kept the details private despite all the rumors and assumptions that had been tossed around behind my back. It just wasn't their business.

But now it really was this detective's business, wasn't it?

But then he'd have questions, and word would get out. I might have become a person of interest in the investigation since this woman effectively broke up my marriage. So I swallowed the whole truth and watched him rub a hand over his face as the elevator dinged and the CSU team filed off the elevator.

"We have to get the guests out of these rooms." He pointed to all the rooms in the hallway. "If not the whole floor."

I nodded, heading down to the lobby to speak with management.

# CHAPTER ELEVEN

## MAYBE I CAN'T HANDLE THE TRUTH

*I SIT WITH MY HANDS OVER MY MOUTH* in shock as I listen to him tell this sick, twisted story that was the end of his fling, the end of my marriage. The death of the woman who tore us apart. I zone out for a while, unable to think, unable to listen to him ramble about how her death affected him, how he couldn't think and had to get out of the department for a while.

When I start to listen again, he's talking about the murders.

"…things became a bit clearer. Turned out she was in the hotel hiding from whoever was harassing her. When we interviewed the family, her mother told us that she decided to get out of her place because someone kept breaking in. Angela never reported anything, maybe because she worked with us? I don't know. Probably embarrassed to have the whole department know what was being done to her. I couldn't help but dig into the case a little. I found out that he was sexually assaulting one woman in the same bed as the woman he had just killed. The profile suggests bloodlust. He gets off on the blood—might be the only way he *can* get off. Sometimes he moves the bodies; sometimes he moves the rape victim. It changes each time. He's less consistent than your typical serial killer that way. They think he does it on purpose to throw us, make him harder to track." He takes a deep breath. "At least that's what Small said. I don't think he really knows. Serial killers don't ever act like this guy does, and he said it's making it hard to figure out."

"You mean he slashed some woman in my bed and then sexually assaulted me in the mess? Then he took the body and left?" I force myself to breathe. "That's where all that blood came from." I say the last bit quietly.

He nods slowly. He looks pale, sick over the knowledge. "I assume so. Just putting two and two together here, but it seems that he got her out in the middle of the night without being seen as well. Your neighbors didn't see or hear a thing."

"Detective Small told you all this?"

"Yes. We did a lot of talking when I called to follow up on the murder. We went to lunch. He's torn up over this case, can't solve it. The chief is tying his hands. He thought maybe new eyes might help him see something he missed, so we did some talking over a few beers a few times. I might not work for the department right now, but I'm still a cop."

I touch a shaking hand to my forehead, finding it damp with sweat. "I feel sick. This truly is real, isn't it?"

I feel like I'm going to throw up. Bolting, I manage to make it to the toilet, just barely, the run giving me a dull headache as I heave up the expensive dinner.

"Holy Jesus, someone really wants to kill me?" I scream from the bathroom between lurches. He comes around the corner to find me sobbing on the bathroom floor, my head resting on the toilet seat.

"You're the first to come forward this early, you know. You could be the key to catching him."

Oh lucky, lucky me.

"I could be number seven!" I lift my head. He sits in a crouch in front of me. "Why me? Why did someone like me catch his attention?"

"I don't know. But we will get through this, together. I wonder if you should really go off by yourself tomorrow, Wren. I'd rather keep you close by."

"I can't. I need my job!" I whine, blowing my nose in a wad of toilet paper. "*If* I live, I'd rather not do it in prison."

"Come to bed. I'll hold you until you calm down." He gets to his feet, holding out a hand for me. I look up, taking it after a moment.

"How can I calm down? This is horrible. How can someone be like that? What sick twist in someone's head makes them like that?" I sniffle as I'm led out of the bathroom and to the bedroom. I don't say anything about his assumption that being in his arms might calm me down; at this juncture, who cares?

"I don't know. I'd rather not think about that too much. I'll save my energy for you and figuring out how to keep you safe and helping Small find out who this is once and for all." He gets one of his T-shirts out and lays it on the bed. When he reaches for the buttons on my blouse, I smile through my tears.

"Are you undressing me?"

"Yes."

I laugh, wiping my eyes as his fingers work the buttons one by one, slipping the shirt from my shoulders. Pants next. He winks at me, now in my underwear as he tosses my clothes into his laundry basket. "Bra." He snaps his fingers, grabbing the shirt from the bed.

He's already seen me naked a million times over, so I shrug and figure why not. I slip it off, and he smiles as I pull his shirt over my head.

"Get into bed."

I meet his eyes and don't know what to say. It's only been days, and everything has changed. It's upside down, my entire life, as if it's a book and some author is itching to type *The End* on the page, snuffing me out.

But no, not me. I won't go lightly into this darkness. It's not my time. It can't be.

So many thoughts in the span of a second, I struggle to refocus on him. Ricky. I see everything in his gentle expression. This man carries his passion on his sleeve, his heart in everything he does. He bends, kissing me on the mouth before he settles down, reaching for me. I relax against his chest, in his arms, and fall into sleep without fighting him just this once. I need this, even if it's false, fake, even if the peace is a pretense. I'll take anything.

*** *** ***

Sleep that starts out peaceful doesn't end that way. I wake over and over throughout the night from dreams that I can't really remember but that haunt me just the same. Broken pieces of them drift into my consciousness every time I wake, but that's all, and I wonder if it's a gift from God. Maybe I just can't handle it. Maybe he's taking it easy on me for once, just this once.

By morning, I'm exhausted, more so than I was before bed. I wake at four because I have to be at the airport soon. I'm careful not to wake Ricky up when I climb out of bed, but when I get out of the bathroom, I smell coffee and know that he's awake. For me.

I want to cry. What if he has to watch me die too? Am I being selfish not to want to spend what might be my last days alone? And what if I don't die? Can Ricky and I be us again, or is what he did too much?

I walk down the hall and find him moving around the kitchen in his pajamas, hair sticking up all over. I smile at the sight.

"I promise I'll be careful."

After we've eaten breakfast and I'm ready to head out the door, I start to gather my luggage.

"What are you thinking?" he says as he walks into the living room, pulling a shirt over his head before buttoning his jeans. "Uber? Yeah, no. I'm taking you to the airport. Let's go." He slips on a pair of flip-flops and grabs my luggage from my hand before I can answer him.

The goodbye at the airport is a slew of promises that I'll call and be careful, all under the awkward, watchful eye of Doug, who stands far enough away so that it seems like he's giving us our space, but I know he's probably listening. Ricky tells me that I should consider telling him what's going on, but I know I won't. No way.

On the plane. Buckled in. It's done. Doug sits beside me, and I wonder when it's okay for me to put in my headphones and listen to an audiobook that I got just for this flight, hoping he won't try to chat with me for two hours. I'm too nervous to talk.

All my feelings are in one oozing knot floating around in my gut right now. I try not to think about the rest of the day, or last night, or anything else, but it proves impossible.

# CHAPTER TWELVE

## THE BOSS

IT'S BEEN A WHILE SINCE I FELT THE need to check in with someone. On top of that, I had to get express written permission from Alex to even be legally allowed to take this trip. Even as a kid after Mom died, I rarely checked in or asked for permission, feeling like I was an afterthought. I might have been their granddaughter, but I wasn't meant to be there, so I just sort of *was*. I didn't come home high or pregnant or get arrested, so I was doing okay in their book, I suppose. Now I have to check in with a probation officer, and my husband is expecting to hear from me, but I only text one of them when I get here.

After the flight, sitting in the back of a cab beside Doug, I message Ricky to tell him I arrived safely. He's at work, but he replies within a few minutes with **I'm thinking of you**. I don't much care for Ricky's crap, so instead of answering, I pocket my phone and try to remember that I'm hundreds of miles away from this supposed killer and from Ricky. I should be able to relax here. Forget them both.

Doug's room is right across from mine, of course. He walks me into my room and sets my bags on the bed, then turns with wide-open arms as if presenting some grand prize. I laugh at him; he winks and I shake my head. "It's a marvelous room, right? Only the best."

I glance around. It's a good room, no doubt, but it's not anything spectacular. "It's nice enough. Calm down," I dare to tease. Might as well try to relax. I've never been anything but professional with him, but here in California and not in the office, I guess I can be a bit more myself—whatever is left of me after all this, anyway.

"I know it's not home, but it's still pretty good. I brought your laptop. Here."

He pulls out a flat black bag from the pile on the bed and removes a smooth gray laptop. He tells me the generic password and then proceeds to spend half an hour showing me this and that. We go over the schedule again, and he shows me his notes for the first session. I'm supposed to go with him to help him during the sessions and keep him organized. I've got access to my email, his email, and when it's all said and done, he hands me an iPhone wrapped in a black Otter Box and tells me it's my work phone. Calls from the office will be forwarded so I can handle anything. We're currently in the middle of a case, so there may be a lot of them. I hope I can handle them, because all I am is an assistant, a glorified secretary, not a paralegal.

I palm the phone and look up at him. "Wow, thanks. All this just for this trip?"

His eyes are warm when he glances over his shoulder at me, shutting the laptop. "We'll see. I'm inclined to let you keep them so you can check in during off hours and I don't miss any important messages, especially during big cases like this one, but that would constitute a raise. That's more work."

He sits on the bed, cocking his head to one side. He looks good for a man twenty years older than I am. His ice-blue eyes sparkle as he leans back casually on his hands, accented by a hint of crow's feet. His dark brown hair has a sprinkle of gray.

"Well, I appreciate you considering me, sir." A raise would be nice, even if it does mean more work.

He laughs, a warmer sound than I'm used to. Maybe because we're essentially in a bedroom together? "Wren, don't call me 'sir.' Not here. Okay?"

"You mean in California?"

He stands up, inches taller than I am, forcing my eyes up. "That too."

He grins at me, and suddenly I realize what he means. In here, the hotel room. My insides twist, and I don't know what to say. But he doesn't say anything, so I don't either. Maybe he didn't mean to be obvious. Perhaps he's just goofing around; I don't really know what kind of guy he is outside of work, after all.

"Let's meet up in an hour and go get something to eat, see the sights, you know? Dress comfortably for now. We'll come back to change again before the evening starts."

He walks out the door, and I can breathe again. Shit, anything can happen in four days. And honestly, I'm starting to think he's not actually as bad as I thought.

I shower the plane nasties off me, then change into shorts and a hoodie and redo my face. After I call Ricky and get his voice mail, I check my Snapchat messages and see I have two. I open Lily's with a smile, finding her face covered with a silly filter, her fingers in a V in front of her face with her tongue stuck between them. I roll my eyes and chuckle as I read her message.

**Let me know how it goes… hope you like old man balls… hahahahaha**

I make a gagging face and send it back to her with a message. **Omg! You're nuts! (Get it… nuts?) bahaha**

Before I can get back to the other message, Doug knocks on my door. I close the app and shove my phone into my purse.

Upon opening the door, I catch his eyes drift down my legs and back up; it's quick, but I notice. For a moment, I wonder if I'm too comfortable. Maybe I should have worn something else. But when I look up, I see he's wearing loose jeans and a Guns N' Roses T-shirt with a baseball cap.

"Ready?" He smiles.

As ready as I'll ever be, I guess.

By the time I'm back at the hotel changing into a suit and heels, I've had a great time with him. He's easy to talk to and funny; plus he's warm and nice, not the skeez I thought he was, that it's rumored he is. I actually like him. I learned that he's been married twice, once when he was eighteen for a year and again at twenty-three, and he was married to her for twenty years and had two kids. They got divorced after years of growing apart. He's been single for three years. He spends his weekends fishing, of all things. Don't know what I expected, but that wasn't it.

I ended up talking a lot too, in between the listening. I got the feeling that it's been a while since he had someone to really talk to, though I'm not sure why. I told him about my mom and growing up with my grandparents and kind of just feeling like a piece of furniture at times. Out of place with two old people— an old woman who didn't think twice about offering me cigarettes and coffee and an old man who lived in his "workshop" all day long. I wasn't neglected; it was just… not Mom.

As he listened, he looked at me with those icy-blue eyes and made me wonder why I was telling him so much.

By the time orientation was over and we were sitting around laughing at lawyer jokes with four other strangers at dinner, I kind of wished I had told him the truth. All of it, even the bit about my almost certain impending doom.

So now it's almost eight as we ride up the elevator in silence, my heels in one hand, suit jacket in the other. He has his jacket over one arm when the doors open, waving for me to go first with the other.

I've got my new backpack on my shoulder, as does he, the one we got at check-in before orientation, loaded with little doodads and a folder full of papers I've only glanced at.

It's in this moment that I realize I fully forgot all about the work phone. I stop walking, and my eyes go wide. *Shit. There goes that raise.* I open my purse, seeing him turn to watch me out of the corner of my eye as I search for it, but it's not there.

"Shit, I forgot it," I mutter.

"What?"

"The phone. I forgot. I was having fun and I just forgot."

He grins, his eyes laughing before he does, and shakes his head at me. "It's okay. We'll go in and check together. I forgot too."

He holds out a hand for me, an invitation. Confusion washes over me, and time slows down in that split second that I have to decide what to do.

Just a hand. Just a simple friendly gesture. Nothing else. I'm separated, not promised to anyone. I might not even live to see next week.

I swallow the saliva pooled in my mouth and then step forward, taking the offered hand. It's cool and wraps around mine, seemingly unpresuming. He pulls me to the door and holds his other hand out for my key, which I slap into his palm, smirking when he opens the door and gently shoves me inside.

"Don't fire me." I laugh, flipping on the light.

"We'll see. Where's the phone?"

I look down, noticing missed calls and messages. I flush, tossing my shoes down and opening a drawer for a pad and a paper. "Damn."

It takes about an hour or so to get through the messages, return calls and emails, and then listen to him scold me with a playful glint in his eye as I sit cross-legged on the hotel bed while he paces.

"I have to say, I had a hell of a good time today," he says at the end of his lecture.

My face grows warm, and I look toward the window, then back toward my personal phone, knowing Ricky is waiting on my call. "Me too. I really did."

Ricky can wait.

Our eyes meet across the space between us, and the question hangs unspoken.

What now?

I know he's thinking it; it's all over his face. He tries to hide it, but his eyes give him away. He knows I know too, based on the slow smile that creeps over his lips, pulling them upward as he crosses his arms over his chest.

"Are you tired?" he finally asks me.

Am I? I shrug. "I don't know." Sometimes I don't

until I finally lie down and realize that I was exhausted. "But I need to make a phone call."

He nods. "Well, if you want to watch a movie on TV or something, text me and I'm up for it, okay?"

"Sure. What time is breakfast?"

"We have to be there at eight thirty, so let's meet up at seven thirty."

"Okay."

He walks out, and I jump up and lock my door, turn on my TV, and collapse on the bed. I call Ricky and spend almost an hour on the phone with him, forgetting the confusion that Doug has stirred up by the time I hang up. I spend half of the call assuring him that I'm fine, actually having a good time, and that it's really nice not to be freaking out for a minute.

His soft "Good night" echoes in my head and warms me deep inside just like it used to, and I have to tell myself that we aren't us anymore. He made his bed, and I'm no longer interested in being in it.

I open Snapchat and find Lily, sending her a new selfie of me lying on the bed. **He's not nearly as bad as we heard he was. Nice, fun guy!**

Her reply is instant. I caught her online. **OOOH do you like him? You craving something older?**

**Me: No, just saying. He's fun to be around. Get your mind out of the gutter, woman.**

**Lily: I can't, my mind stays in the gutter.**

**Me: I know. Good night, you slut.**

**Lily: LOL, slut yourself. I predict you will be in his bed by the end of the week.**

**Me: Fuck off... LOL.**

I exit her chat and remember the other one I've ignored all day, completely forgotten. I don't recognize the screenname, Eqd27, but I open the chat anyway. There's no picture, just a message.

**Hey, I know I know you from somewhere. Where did you go to high school?**

I furrow my brow and click on the profile. It's just an artsy picture of a man's shoes. Okay then. I go back to the chat, wondering if it's spam.

**Me: Miller Brook High School, I graduated in 2012.**

**Eqd27: That's not it. I saw your picture. You're really pretty, but damn if I don't know you from someplace. It's bugging the hell out of me. Is Wren your real name?**

**Me: Yeah. Would help if I knew your name, lol.**

**Eqd27: My name is Brian. I guess it will eventually come to me.**

**Me: I'm sure. Maybe I just look**

`like someone you know.`

`  Eqd27: I guess that could be, but I don't think so. Here, I'll send you a picture. Maybe you will remember me, 'cause it's going to drive me nuts until I figure out why you seem so familiar.`

The picture. Fuck me.

I start to shake as I stare at it.

It's him. The killer.

Oh God.

I stare, unable to look away, at a picture of myself, but this time I'm not alone. This time, there's a man in the bed between me and another woman, but he's altered his face with black scribbles so I can't see it. He's naked, one hand holding the phone, positioned for the sickest selfie of all time, and the other hand has a knife in it. There's blood everywhere, and her, she's dead. Slashed, white and bleeding, eyes wide and vacant.

I scream, loud and long, dropping my phone as if the image might come to life again. I'm still screaming when Doug bursts into my room, breaking the lock and splintering the door in the process, looking around like he's ready to take on whatever is in here with me.

The killer found me again. He's not finished.

# CHAPTER THIRTEEN

## SELFIE

I THINK I FAINTED. I'VE NEVER fainted. Blinking, I struggle to sit up, my head a full throb. Doug hovers over me, kneeling beside me in my bed, a look of complete confusion all over his face. "Shit, Wren, what happened? Are you okay?"

I look around. There's no one else here. No killers or cops or anyone. No other guests coming to check and see why someone screamed. That figures.

"Yeah. Damn. Yeah, I'm okay. I can't believe I fainted."

He helps me to my feet. "You have a concussion, don't you? Do I need to get you to a doctor? Why did you scream?"

What do I say? Something stupid like I saw a spider? No, I'm not that girl.

I swallow, then get up and try to shut the door. "You broke the door, Hercules." I turn when it won't fit back in the doorframe.

"What was I supposed to do, knock? You were screaming like Ted Bundy was in here or something." He flops down on the bed, waiting for an explanation.

"Ted Bundy, huh? Funny you should say that." I sigh, not seeing any other options. I have to tell him the truth. At least some of it. "I can't stay in this room."

"Obviously. I'll call them in a minute. Now what's going on?"

I sit beside him and take a deep breath. In one long breath, I tell him about the SMS Killer, about me and what happened. I can't bring myself to show him the picture, but then I remember that Snapchats disappear, so I open my phone and screenshot the conversation before it vanishes. I make sure he's not looking when I do it, and I notice that after the picture is another message. I start crying when I read it.

**You were a great fuck. Can't wait to see you again, baby. Xoxo.**

"Jesus. Why me?" I whisper. I can't stop the tears. "He's going to find me."

I look up at Doug, and he's got this stunned look on his face that makes me wonder if he's going to up and run out on me. Who would blame him?

"Have you called the police?" he finally asks.

"Yes, though I didn't even want to at first. I don't know what to do. I can't imagine that he knows where I am right now, but he'll find me again. I'm sure of it."

"Then you have to be ready when he does. *If* he does."

"How? He drugged me both times. I'm not even sure how he did it. I assume he copied my keys or something after the club, but I haven't been staying at home. No one knows where I am except a couple of people. How do I defend myself against that?"

"I don't know. You can't be alone, that much is obvious."

"That's impossible."

"Well, you can try. Between me and Ricky, we can cover you until the police catch him."

And just like that, I'm caught between two men. How does that even happen to someone like me?

I swallow, then turn to find a place to sit. He leans over and grabs the phone, calling the desk and explaining what happened, offering to pay for the damage.

"They don't have any more rooms," he tells me when he hangs up the phone. "The conference has the place booked. My room has double beds though, so you can stay with me."

I'll have to, I guess. "Okay, let me get my stuff."

He sits by while I gather up what little I've unpacked while I think about what to do. If I tell Ricky, he'll want me to come home. I know the police need to see the message before it's deleted, so on a whim, I grab my purse and find the card that Detective Small gave me. I wonder if he'd tell Ricky. Pulling my phone out, I text him.

**Don't tell Ricky. I'm out of**

**town and don't want to freak him out.**

I send the pictures, and he immediately calls me. I spend a few minutes answering his questions and listening to his promise that he won't say a word, then explain that I'll tell Ricky when I get home. He claims to understand, saying something about Ricky being too close to this and that he would jump the gun and hop on a plane to come get me.

I ask him about the woman, the dead one in the bed. He doesn't really answer me, just gives me this vague bullshit I'm sure he feeds everyone. I let it go, for my own sanity.

I think I'm doing the right thing. It's not like I'm alone. But if I'm wrong, I might be the dead one in the next selfie.

The TV is on *Shark Tank* in Doug's room when I join him, and there's a half-empty beer on the table in front of him.

"You have beer?" I ask, unsure of where to put my stuff.

He laughs, pointing to the bed closest to the window. "Yeah, I went down and got some earlier. You want one?"

"Yes, yes I do. But I'm not supposed to drink."

He cracks one open, then holds it back with a raised eyebrow when I reach for it. "Why?"

"I'm on probation for DWI. Onetime deal. I drove drunk and hit a police car."

He narrows his eyes at me.

"Don't fire me."

He rolls his eyes, handing me the drink. I put the cold bottle to my lips, the golden liquid not enough to numb me but enough to give me a twinkle of hope for some stress relief.

"Do you even have a driver's license anymore?"

I shake my head, swallowing a mouthful. "No, suspended for now. I'll get it back eventually."

Our eyes meet, and he finally smiles. "Why didn't you tell me?"

"You could have fired me, and I need this job. If I lose my job, I could go to jail."

He flops down on the bed, propped up on pillows, beer in his hand. "So what you're saying is I've got you by the balls."

I laugh, grabbing my bag and pulling out shorts and a shirt to sleep in. "I don't have balls."

"No, no you sure don't."

I catch the tone but don't say anything. It's flirtatious, laced with unspoken innuendo.

When I glance up, his eyes are on the TV, not on me. I grab my clothes and head to the bathroom to change.

When I come back out, I don't know what to say. It doesn't seem like it could have been me in that picture, but it was. Strange to see yourself in an image you don't remember, especially something that would be in a horror movie. It's burned into my brain; I wish I could erase it, but I know it'll be stuck there forever.

I'll never be rid of it. My mind races, wondering what to say to Doug, when to tell Ricky, how to save my own life—too many questions with no answers.

Maybe Doug senses that it's best to leave me be and not mention my fit, the fainting, the end of my life. He just lies there, occasionally glancing when I move my stuff, finish the beer, and crawl into the bed, hugging the extra pillow with my eyes on the TV, not really seeing it.

All I can think about is dying and what I should be doing if I really only have a little while left. How do you live when you know your number might be up? Will I know when it hits me, or will he drug me? Will I look into the eyes of my killer and gasp my last breath or just wake up dead?

I need to stop thinking about it, but I don't know how.

Eventually I start to yawn, my eyes getting heavy. Sleep takes me soon after.

That feeling of being smothered finds me in my dreams. I feel wet and like something is dripping on my skin. Ice-cold hands touch me. Someone calls me "baby."

I wake, crying, gasping, and realizing I must have been loud because Doug is sitting on the edge of my bed and almost scares me half to death when I first see him. When I can focus, I start to cry harder and try to curl away from him, embarrassed. He doesn't let me, just pulls me up and into his arms. He doesn't demand any explanation, no asking what I dreamed or giving silly childlike promises that it will all be okay. He knows it might not be. He just offers me warm comfort in a moment when I might not want to be left to comfort myself.

I sink into him, not really meaning to, but it just happens. His body heat rolls off him and into me as my tears wet his T-shirt. My arms start out curled between me and him, but as I relax, as the tears stop, they go around him. He pulls me tighter, and I listen to the rhythm of his breathing in the dark, wondering if I should break the silence by saying something.

"I'm sorry I woke you up," I finally whisper.

He rubs my arm. "Don't be. You're going through some stuff, and it's okay."

"No, it's not okay. It's not okay to drag you into this when all you're doing is trying to work."

"It's fine. I think it's safe to call you a friend after you've cried on me." He laughs lightly.

"Or after you've broken my door down."

We both laugh at that. What else can we do? If I don't, then I'll cry. I'll scream, throw a class A hissy fit of a temper tantrum. I'd rather laugh.

"No shit, right?" He chuckles.

We both pull back, and I wipe my face.

I look up into his eyes, bright even in the darkness. I never imagined myself attracted to a man twenty years older, but here I am. Maybe it's that whole *I might be dead in a week* thing. "You didn't think twice about believing me, did you?" I ask.

"Why would I? Who would lie about something like that?"

"Weirdos. Nuts wanting attention. But you just instantly believed me, not a doubt for a second. You don't even seem worried."

He frowns just a little before letting me go. "I am worried, but that won't change anything. I don't want to sit here and interrogate you or make you talk about something so obviously horrible that it's doing this to you. I think just being here is probably the best thing right now. Is that okay?"

"Yes, that's fine."

"Besides, you're a good assistant, and I don't really want to train a new one." He laughs, as do I, smacking his arm playfully.

"Very funny. Go back to sleep."

He stands up and gets back in bed. I roll over with my back to him, still warmed by his embrace, thinking of Doug, of Ricky, of death. I wonder if death really is some dark-robed bogeyman waiting to outstretch a long, bony finger, taking a life with a mere touch.

"Are you okay?" he murmurs.

I take in a deep breath, filling my lungs and blowing it out slowly as I think about how many more times I will get to do that—breathe—before I answer. "No."

He doesn't respond, and I guess we eventually fall back to sleep because the next thing I know, I'm scrambling around him, sharing a single bathroom as we get ready for the day.

# CHAPTER FOURTEEN

## FOUND

"WHAT ABOUT THE MEDIA?" DOUG ASKS as I text Ricky while he stuffs pancakes into his mouth.

"What about them?" I hit Send, watching the three dots pop up as Ricky responds. I can't bring myself to tell him about the selfie, or that I'm now sharing a room with Doug.

"Maybe they can help. What if there are other survivors out there who haven't come forward? That might help catch him. And what about saving someone else? You could save someone who might not otherwise know what to watch for."

I cut a triangle out of my own syrup-soaked pancakes, swirl them in the puddle of melted butter, and stick the fork in my mouth, thinking about what he said.

"But what about my privacy? My business broadcasted all over the world? And the police haven't released a thing."

"That is a mistake. You know I'm right. You lose a little privacy, but imagine all the women you would save. You could be a hero." He waves his fork at me. "You don't need their permission—the police, I mean."

I sip my coffee and think for a moment on what he's saying. One good media blast. Get this guy out there, warn everyone, call for survivors. Call women to band together to get this bastard once and for all before he gets any more of us. "What happens when the police get angry?"

"Nothing. Who cares if they get angry? You're really doing them a big favor. The media does suck, I agree, but they do have a purpose and a place when it comes to something like this. They're the voice that can help you here. Give you the upper hand. This killer, whoever he is, thinks he's got you pinned. This might change that."

I swallow another mouthful before looking up. He's watching me with a frown, but there's hope in his eyes. "It might also really piss him off and make him want to kill me that much faster."

His wrinkled forehead smooths out as his frown flattens. "I guess that's true too." He sighs.

The waitress comes back, refreshes our coffee, and puts the check on the table. He grabs it before I can. I offer to pay, but he rolls his eyes and tells me to forget it.

Our eyes meet across the small space between us

and I flush, remembering how his arms made me feel last night. Then I think of Ricky, who's been taking care of me for days now. But death looms, large and dark over me. I feel no real guilt for my urges, just the ache to keep on living—the desire to fight and keep fighting, even if it doesn't help. At least I won't have just laid down and done nothing.

The question presents itself once more: What does one do when they might be at their end?

Whatever the fuck they want, that's what.

"I guess if it's a possibility no matter what I do, I might as well go out fighting, right? Maybe even help someone else along the way." I start to shovel food into my mouth. Screw my diet. Who cares that I need to lose forty pounds? No one cares about a skinny cadaver. A pretty corpse. I almost laugh at myself on that one as I swirl smoky maple sausage in the leftover syrup and butter before eating it. "I'll call Ricky today and see what he thinks. Maybe we can work on it while we're here. Being a lawyer, you might be the best person to help me."

He nods. "You got it. You won't be alone."

I look up to find him watching me behind his coffee cup. "Okay."

We leave the restaurant and head to the conference center. I help him get everything ready, lots of little things like hanging up the sign, setting up the computers, making sure we have copies and pens, checking to see if everything is working. I go through his email and answer what I can while I wait for things to start, and he goes over his notes. I flag what I can't answer so we can go over it later. I check our voice mail, return calls, schedule appointments, and send things to his paralegal, who's preparing a court case for him, doing all the research and the document gathering.

By the time I get that done, people are filing in. Some are dressed in suits, others casual in jeans and polo shirts. Some carry laptops and legal pads. A few bring nothing. Everyone is different. But it's just like high school, people sitting in clusters and eager beavers taking up the front row. I pass around a sign-up sheet and make sure everyone has the packet prepared in a glossy folder full of information, business cards, and the copy of the PowerPoint presentation.

Once it all begins, I sit back and listen with one ear and stare at my laptop in between glances up at Doug. Snapchat calls to me, the urge to see if he ever messaged me again. The sick desire to know trumping the cold, nauseating fear that grips my guts as I tell myself I will delete my account, or the app, as if that might save me.

Finally I give in, taking out my phone and pulling up the app.

New message from Lily: **So did you get some?**

**Me: Very funny. He's a cool guy, really. And no, I didn't get some.**

I open the message thread from him and my

mouth goes dry. Will he be there? Anything new? Is he watching to see if I'm online? I should delete the app, but it won't help. He'll still find me. I could toss my phone in the garbage, but he knows where I live. Probably knows all about me. Wants to know everything about the life he wants to take away.

There are no new messages. The account is actually gone now, probably thanks to Detective Small. I sigh and close the app, wondering absently what comes next.

I look up, finding Doug lost in his presentation, the audience taking notes. Everything seems to be going well, so I click on my internet browser and start to google "SMS Killer," "known serial killers," and anything else I can think of. I don't find much, just anything you would expect to find when you type "killer" or "serial killer" or "murder" into a search engine. There really is nothing out there about him.

It amazes me that so little is known. Typically the media is all over serial killers. But I suppose my hope makes it hard for me to swallow the fact that there have been no reported survivors, no case studies, no crowds up in arms that so much has been swept under the rug. On the other hand, I can understand why no one would want to call the police, especially since I only did when my hand was forced. Maybe someone did. Perhaps one of them was braver than I was, or their circumstances were different. Maybe they reported everything and died anyway. Who's to say he stays in one place?

Maybe he jumps around or something. There's just so much I don't know. So many questions that no one knows the answer to, no one but a killer and a bunch of dead women.

In that moment, I decide I have to do this. I have to alert the media. The world. Let women know what's happening and what the police are keeping from them. How dare they let their agenda and personal feelings keep them from protecting the world?

The more I think about it, the angrier I get. By the time the session is over, I'm ready to call the chief's office and give him hell.

"How did I do?" Doug plops down next to me when the last person has left and we're alone.

I smile at him. "Great. I was impressed. You sound like you really know what you're talking about up there."

He grins. "Thanks. I don't have another one until later this afternoon. Wanna get out of here?"

"Yes, let's go."

In the car, he asks me if I want to go see Alcatraz, and I say yes before he can even finish the sentence. He laughs at me, and I relax enough to tell him what I decided.

"I'm going to do it, talk to the media. It's my best weapon at this point. Will you help me?" I look at him, hoping my expression isn't too pleading.

He reaches over and puts his hand on my thigh. It's warm through my suit pants. A week ago, I would have balked, but now it's a welcome touch. I feel like we've connected on a deeper level than just boss and employee.

"Of course. We can work on it tonight."

"Great. I just want to forget about it for a while."

"I'll see what I can do." His hand remains, gives me a gentle squeeze.

We tour the old prison, and frankly, it's amazing. I gush about it all through lunch. We have chowder at a stand on Fisherman's Wharf, and then he buys me a couple souvenirs. We take some pictures; I pull him close for a selfie with the water behind us.

It's that moment when I look at him that I know. He meets my eyes with that smile, and the faint sound of the sea lions comes from the distance. It doesn't happen like I expected. He doesn't grab me and kiss me; rather I lean in and touch my lips to his, gripping his button-down shirt in both hands to pull him closer. He responds with an open mouth and a sigh, offering his tongue to me. I accept it as he takes my face in his hands and kisses me with the same want that I have for him. I thought it would feel strange to kiss someone else, someone who isn't Ricky, but it doesn't. Not sure if that's good or bad; though in this moment, I don't really care.

The ache to crawl onto his lap and straddle him is almost more than I can take. I want him, want to take him back to the hotel and ask him to touch me. To arch under his touch, to feel life pulsing through me in an orgasm that threatens to break me. But I don't. I kiss him, deep and long, and then I pull away from him with a moan and an acute throb between my legs that begs to be comforted.

I think of Ricky. He didn't care, didn't think of me while he had his dick in that woman, did he? As much as I'd love to throw caution to the wind in the name of "I might die," in this moment, I decide not to.

"What about your husband?" he asks me, studying my face with his hand still in my hair.

I owe him the truth, so I give it to him. I tell him about the rumors at work, the way Ricky and I have been separated due to his infidelity, the whole nine yards. I can't gauge his reaction by his expression, so I wait.

"You want to know what really happened?" he starts. "Last Christmas party, Lily and I did hook up. It was a one-night, drunken thing, and I regretted it after. She's the only one I've touched. She told a bunch of people, and it turned into this twisted tale. I think she was trying to cover her own ass by making me look like a womanizer. That's probably why she keeps teasing you, hoping it'll happen with someone else and make her version true. Or look true, anyway. I'm not like that; it was just one of those things. Of course, you don't have to believe me."

"I believe you. I hang out with her, but we aren't close. I just heard rumors. She never told me anything, and I didn't ask."

"I understand. The rumor annoyed me more than anything. I guess it was my own fault for letting it happen." He smiles, though it's somewhat subdued. "We need to head back to the conference."

"Let's go."

That night we sit huddled over the computer with beer and chips, *Shark Tank* once again on the TV, but we aren't watching. We're too busy scripting the media blast—what to say, what not to say.

"Don't make the police look bad. Just state the facts and let people draw their own conclusions," he says, pointing to a line.

I delete it and replace it with a new phrase.

"You think this will really help?" I stare at the completed draft. It's almost ten now. We're down to one beer left in the six-pack we picked up on the way back.

"I think so. You think you can read it without getting stage fright?"

"I hope so. Do I need a lawyer or anything?"

"No, I don't think so. I can go for show, if you want. Be supportive."

"Maybe so. I'll tell Ricky about it when we get back, see what he thinks. I was going to tell him before we got back, but I changed my mind; he would ask too many questions. But I think he'll go for it too. It's a good idea." I think for a moment. "How will we get them to show up? The news people?"

"Leave that to me. I'll handle it. Nothing suspicious

today?" He leans back on the bed beside me.

I close the laptop and put it on the nightstand. "No, just a message from my PO. I need to call her back, but it's too late. I texted her when we got back, so that'll be enough for now. I'll call in the morning. Thanks for your help, Doug."

It happens slowly, after I thank him. The eye contact, closing in, the first touch of warm lips that taste of salty chips and cold beer. Soon it's a deep kiss that moves down my neck, a leg tossed over his hips, and a hand drifting up the skin of my thigh. The air around us fills with the sounds of panting and gentle moans, coupled with body language that begs to be taken. My shirt falls on the floor and his mouth moves on my body, my hands pulling him closer. I throw my legs wide when his fingers start to move up my leg, between them, breaking the barrier of my loose shorts and touching the already wet edge of my panties. I whimper and gasp, and then swear when my phone rings.

Because of the time, where I am, and what's happening, I know I need to at least see who's calling. It's Detective Small.

My heart stops beating for a moment as flashes of hell pass before my eyes in the split second that it takes to reach for my phone and Doug to roll off me. Maybe they caught him. Maybe it's not bad news.

I reach for the phone with one eye on him, on how his chest rises and falls with rapid breaths, not quite panting. The other eye's on the phone, steeling myself for whatever might be coming. It's going to be big, whatever it is.

"Hello." I try not to sound out of breath.

"Wren, hope I didn't wake you up."

"No, I was awake. I haven't been sleeping all that great."

"I bet. I wanted to let you know that the woman in the selfie you sent me yesterday… we found her."

I sit up, pulling the covers up to cover my bare breasts, then realize that I was holding my breath when I have to let it go to speak. My heart is a dull, slow throb, as if the news set me into slow motion. "Was she alive?"

He breathes out a sigh. "No, no she wasn't. I think you know from the picture that she would be very dead."

"It's been weeks. Where was she?"

"She must have been kept in a cooler or something, because she was in good shape. She was found out in the open like the last one. Judging from what we now know from you, I think he holds on to them for a while before he dumps them."

I don't want to think about what that means. I feel my gag reflex stir as the dark imaginings invade my mind against my will. "What does that mean for me?"

"Well, based on this, the time between deaths seems to span anywhere from six weeks to three months. The older cases took longer, as is usually the case. As they progress, they need faster gratification. It's been about three weeks since your first contact, so I'd say—"

"Three weeks." I breathe the words as I close my eyes.

"Could be longer."

*Could be*, not *will be*. Maybe. He's going to be hungry. He's done away with his last toy and needs a new one.

I swallow, closing my eyes to the tunnel vision that threatens to steal my consciousness in another faint. "Oh my God," I say to no one, to everyone. To God, to the Devil, anyone who might listen. "He's going to fucking kill me, isn't he?"

"Not if we can help it. We have the upper hand here."

"The hell you do. How can you have the upper hand when you have no idea what's really coming?" I almost yell, suddenly trembling. I reach for my shirt, pulling it over my head with my phone still in hand. "I'm going to the media," I blurt.

"I think that might be a good idea. Let me know when you get back home. We'll set you up with protection."

"How can you protect me when you don't know who you're protecting me from?"

"Trust me, Wren. We know what we're doing."

"Like you did with the last six—seven now? Oh God… shit. Three weeks," I mutter, hanging up on him, dropping the phone with shaking hands.

I feel as if the color has drained from my face,

and I'm both cold and hot at the same time. There's a deadline stamped on my life, a gravestone cast with my name on it. I'm a bet, a gamble. Will she die? Like one of those office bets: pick a date and time and win the pot!

*I'm going to die.*

The urge to get up and run is almost too great to ignore. Just pack up and go, go until no one can find me. Start over, be someone else. Someone who won't end up as a special on *Investigation Discovery* or *Dateline*.

"Hey." Doug's voice is rich and soft, and I almost don't hear it. It's his hand, the feel of his flesh pressed gently to mine, that wakes me from this nightmare playing in my head for a moment. "Hey, tell me."

I look over into blue eyes laced with concern as he sits on the bed, hand on my cheek.

Why not? What's the point of a secret when you…? I let the thought fizzle out instead of finishing it. Then I lay it out for him with a deep quake in my voice.

"You won't die." He shakes his head. "You won't."

"You can't know that."

"I can believe it, and I do. We'll go to the media as soon as we get back and open this whole thing up. You will live, and they will catch him."

I breathe in the words, hoping they might infect me with his abandon, his hope, his lack of absolute heart-stopping terror. It doesn't really work. All I can think of is what that moment might be like, when I look up into my killer's face and he pushes the knife into my body for the first time. Will it hurt? Will I just go to sleep as I bleed out? Peaceful or panic? What is it like to face the reaper?

I can't keep thinking like this. It'll consume me, throw me into madness. I have to shake this off, find a way to get past it. Something else to focus on. "That makes her number seven, doesn't it? I'd be number eight now," I mumble.

Doug blows out a breath. "I don't think there's really anything I can say to you right now to make this better, but I won't leave you to face this alone, okay?"

I move, sitting up on my knees and pushing myself into his arms. His hug calms me as he tightens his arms around me, his chest strong under mine, my head on his shoulder in the dark. The man I almost had sex with only minutes ago. My boss, now my friend.

I would say something stupid like "It's funny how fast things can change," but I won't let the cliché past my lips.

# CHAPTER FIFTEEN

## CAN OF WORMS

*NOTHING ELSE HAPPENED BETWEEN THAT* night and when I got home—not with the killer or with Doug. He was a support, a hard body to lean on, that's all. By the time I get back and see Ricky, I'm so emotionally exhausted that as soon as I lay eyes on him, it's a real struggle not to just sit on the floor and start bawling. I have so much I need to tell him, but the urge to run away is almost greater.

But not quite.

I know my next step, the only way I can hope to gain the upper hand. I tell Ricky, Doug, and Detective Small to be at Ricky's house for brunch on Saturday morning at ten thirty. I tell Doug to plan the media release for that afternoon at three, just before the evening news. I spend my hours on Thursday and Friday practicing in front of the mirror when no one is around, hoping and praying that I won't look like a fool in front of the whole world.

On Saturday morning as I make brunch, I feel like the detective in one of those old British movies where everyone is invited into the parlor for coffee and dessert while they reveal who the real killer is. I make bacon, a breakfast casserole, a pot of coffee, and a Bundt cake for dessert. Ricky has been asking me what's going on, but I told him to wait. I'm not prepared to answer the same questions over and over again or face the "why did you plan this with him and not me" crap. I just don't have time to worry about any of that right now.

At the appointed time, everyone is here and has coffee in hand, sitting down at the table that Ricky set for me. I sit down, straightening out invisible wrinkles in my khakis as I glance at three sets of male eyes, two of which don't seem to want to make eye contact with one another.

Like a Band-Aid, right? Just do it.

I take in a few deep breaths and just dive right in, no real idea of what to say or how to say it until I'm already speaking.

"I appreciate you all coming. It's just easier to do this all at once, you know? Ricky, some things happened while I was gone, but I didn't want to worry you while I was so far away." I tell him about the Snapchat, calling Detective Small, the dead woman, everything. I leave the press conference until the end, wondering what the reaction will be and not caring much at the same time.

After I let the cat out of the bag, I glance at three

sets of eyes, each also looking around the table, seeming to be waiting for someone else to go first. I pull a folded paper out of my pocket and lay it on the table, open. It's my speech for the conference, retyped and organized with a list of possible media questions at the end. Detective Small is the first to grab it, beating Ricky by a hair.

"Doug helped me write it, made sure I didn't say anything stupid to get anyone into trouble. But this has to be done."

Small's aging, round face furrows as he reads. "I agree, it does need to be done. Chief isn't going to be happy, but he can't stop you." He hands it to Ricky. "Are you her lawyer?" He directs his question to Doug, sitting beside him.

"No, I'm her boss. We handle employment law, but I know my way around a press release. We wrote this, and I helped her send off the press release yesterday."

Ricky hands it back to me. "You could have called me; I would have come to help," he says with a stony face.

I feel flushed, hoping the crimson doesn't bloom on my face. "I know, but I didn't want you to worry."

He shakes his head, redirecting his attention to buttering a biscuit. "It's nothing. You know I'd do whatever it takes to keep you safe. I think the press conference is a good idea." His short eye contact tells me that he would have liked to be more involved, and the side glance at Doug says he's jealous. But he won't say anything.

I swallow a bite of food without really tasting it. "Well, you can all come sit with me—the more company the better. I've never done anything like this and hope I don't mess it all up once I see all those faces and cameras."

The conversation dies out, and after lunch we all agree to meet up at the conference hall and stand together, which comforts me.

Ricky closes the door after our guests leave, locking it behind them. I find my heart in my throat, wondering what he'll say to me when he turns around. He has a right to his questions, but only a little. It's only been a few days, and being thrust together in the gaping maw of death is not what you would call a great way to deal with marital issues.

Instead of waiting for him to turn, I head into the kitchen to clean up. I see his shape approach out of the corner of my eye, but I bend and open the dishwasher, then turn on the sink faucet and squirt soap into the sponge. What comes now? The questions I've been expecting since I got back about Doug or jealousy that he didn't get to help plan the conference? I wipe the sponge over the dish, washing off bits of food and trying not to meet his eyes. He leans on the counter beside me. I stuff the plate into the rack, then stand and reach for another.

"Are you okay, Wren?" His voice is gentle, concerned—not thick with anger or jealousy, not stifled with hidden emotions. It's genuine worry.

I stop rubbing the dish and look at him. No words come out of my mouth. They're screaming in my head, but my lips are clamped tight.

*No, I am not okay. What if I die? I almost slept with Doug. I really like him too. What if this killer finds me? What if this conference gets me killed?*

"You've been quiet since you got back."

My eyes and nose start to burn, and there's a lump forming in my throat as water blurs my vision. I can only get one thing out, not all the other shit that's fighting for space in my head. "I'm going to die, aren't I? A horrible, bloody death. Someone will drain me and dump my body like I'm a bag of trash, won't they? In just a few weeks. That's all I have. Weeks. Why am I standing here doing dishes when my life is over?"

I don't remember throwing the plate, but the next thing I know, it's breaking on the wall and water and soap are dripping down the paint as the pieces crash to the floor. I weep, falling to the ceramic tile, arms around myself as the pain leaks out of me in gut-wrenching sobs.

"You won't die. This isn't it." He kneels beside me, but I don't let him hug me. I don't want anyone's arms around me just now.

"You don't know that." I slap at his hands when he grabs me anyway, pulling me into his chest.

"Neither do you."

He holds me tight, even against my pulling. Soon, I

stop fighting and just cry, not knowing what else to do. I let out all the stuff I've been holding in, trying to be strong and pretend that it's nothing, that it's not bothering me. That I'll be just fine.

It is bothering me.

I am not just fine.

"We will stop him. *You* will stop him. The media might just change everything," he whispers fiercely into my ear.

With no point in talking about it further, I sniffle and whimper a couple more minutes, then do my best to pull myself together. I thank him, accept his forehead kiss, and am urged to go rest while he cleans up. So I do.

I lie in my bed, predicting my future—or lack thereof—as I try to sleep. Sleep does come, though it's only a short nap marred by bad dreams.

\*\*\*

Doug set this thing up in a conference room at a downtown hotel so it would be in a neutral place—not that they won't figure out where I work or all those other personal details that we try to hide. The media will dig and find them and then twist them into half-truths, the things they're best at.

He sent out the press release yesterday, short and sweet.

**Seven Dead at the Hand of the SMS Killer.**

It went on, but not much before ending with the date and time, tempting them to show up.

Now I sit at a long table sandwiched between Doug and Ricky, both smartly dressed in suits. I wear my best work suit, my hair pulled into a loose sock bun. My hands are flat on the table because they're trembling and I don't want it to show. I glance up as the doors open and they file in, filling seats, setting up cameras. There are at least a dozen, probably more, strange faces, eager for the dark meat they ache to feed the public.

"Ready when you are," someone calls out, alerting me that they're set up and ready to go.

I look to the guys, first one, then the other. One nods and smiles; the other pats my hand, his eyes telling me he thinks I'll be just fine.

Water. I need water. I pick up a clear glass and sip. It's cold, and I hope it might loosen my tongue so that I sound okay.

"Thank you for coming today." I sound strong, sure. What a relief. "I'm just going to start at the beginning. Almost a month ago, I woke to discover that I had been drugged and sexually assaulted. Roofied, they call it, possibly GHB given to me that night while I was in a club. Statistics suggest that most women don't report it when such things happen to them, and it was true in this case. I went about my life, but then the offender came back. I discovered that the police have been searching for a killer, dubbed the SMS Killer, for over two years now. This person starts with a drugged sexual assault, then bides his time. The man plays with his victims over a course of weeks, returning to them, seeking them out on social media and sending pictures of previous crimes, sending text messages. I've been dealing with this for weeks, and I've been advised that I am the up-and-coming eighth victim. I am next. It's for this reason that I'm reaching out, to warn and alert women. His victims are spread over the county, so it's assumed he's local. We hope to find more women who didn't come forward, who perhaps survived. You might not have realized what's going on because the police have been hesitant to release information to the media. I hope that you will help me save my own life and stop this killer from doing this again. Don't let there be an eighth, or ninth, or tenth victim. I thank you for taking the time to come today and will now accept questions."

I breathe for the first time since I started speaking, I think. Small sits on the sidelines, out of the eye of the camera, nodding slowly. He didn't want to suggest that he was representing the department. He told me that this will force the chief's hand, and their media liaison will have to come up with an answer, release a profile, and do more. The public will demand it. The old country-boy chief who sits on his ass and rolls his eyes at such things will have no other options.

I watch almost every hand shoot into the air, like a dozen second graders who have to go to the bathroom. Doug has agreed to field many of the questions, in the intcrcst of not compromising the investigation with too much detail. "We can't give away everything," he said as he went over things with me in the hotel room. Of course we can't. I know the police will withhold information as a tactic of investigation.

"My name is Doug Larson, and I'm an attorney with Braskell, Heinrich, and Payne. I am not claiming to be Mrs. Addison's attorney, but I'm here as an acting legal advisor. I will be fielding some of your questions. You, in the front in red."

She stands, recording with her phone. "How does he kill his victims?"

"Stabbing." He selects another.

The questions go on, and he fields some and rejects others. Accusations toward the police department are ignored and referred to their liaison. I'm asked for more detail. What happened? How many times has he come back? Will the text messages be released?

Once the conference is over, they continue tossing out questions as we exit the room. "I hope I did the right thing," I mutter as I head to Doug's big black SUV.

Ricky sits with me in the back seat, Small in the front. "It's all going to break loose now."

I swallow, watching the world go by through a darkly tinted window.

Breaking the wall down, getting knowledge to the public is the first step, I think.

I hope.

# CHAPTER SIXTEEN

## HELLO, CHIEF

MONDAY MORNING, I WALK INTO WORK AS usual, soda in one hand, my purse in the other. I fell back into an old habit of soda for breakfast, one I broke a while back. But when death is looming, who cares?

I take a breath as I walk off the elevator and pull open the glass doors that mark my office. I pass through reception with a weak smile, the receptionist who I often chat with during the day looking up at me with wide, unsmiling eyes. He returns my "Good morning" with a nod.

The bullpen is down the hall, where all the secretaries and paralegals work in cubicles. I'm grateful for the cubicle walls that hide me, sure that many of my coworkers saw me on TV. Others heard about it, or will hear about it. It'll be old news by lunchtime.

I set my soda down, toss my bag into the bottom drawer of my filing cabinet, and sit down. Turning on my computer, I try to get to work.

An IM pops up on my computer. Lily.

**Lily: Why didn't you tell me? You could have told me.**

**Me: I didn't tell anyone. I didn't know it was so serious.**

**Lily: Rape isn't serious?**

I don't know what to say to her. So many questions. So many wrong decisions on my part. What might have happened if I'd gone to the police early on? Probably nothing, but we'll never know.

**Me: I screwed up. I figured it was my fault, you know? I didn't know.**

She doesn't answer. Maybe she's busy, or maybe she thinks I'm full of shit, or lying, or trying to get attention. I minimize the chat and return to my email just long enough to read one when my phone rings. It's Doug.

"Yes, Mr. Larson. Good morning."

"Morning, Wren. Can you come here, please?"

I toss out a "Yes, sir" and stand up, pen and paper in hand, just in case.

Down the hall, left turn. His door is closed. I don't knock, putting my hand on the knob and turning, pausing a beat when I see the back of a police officer in the chair in front of Doug's desk. A broad back, not one of muscle but one of fat.

I swallow, closing the door behind me. The click

and Doug's eyes on me cause the man to turn.

He's in his fifties, maybe, with a deep tan and lines around his eyes. He stands and I see he's well over six feet tall and holds a cowboy hat in his hand. Explains his flat, sweaty blond hair. Green eyes consider me without kindness, even though he offers me a polite smile.

"Wren, this is Chief Mike Mitchell. Have a seat."

In all the time Ricky worked for the department, I never met this man. He was like a shadow. A children's story that all the cops talk about, but you never actually see him anywhere. A desk-bound chief who has his finger in everything from a safe distance, that way he doesn't get dirty but still controls the show.

I don't move for a moment, telling my feet not to turn and run as they seem to want to do. I smile once the shock dies down. Got to be smart, sure of myself here. It's my life on the line, not his.

"Nice to meet you, ma'am," he drawls. He's a stereotype, this guy. I didn't think people like this existed outside of bad movies. The only thing missing is the toothpick hanging out of his mouth. What a joke. "I thought we might have a chat."

I glance between the men. "Nice to meet you," I lie. "I assume you're here because of the press?"

He nods, sitting back down. "I am. The media is at the station, and they're expecting me to make a statement. I don't like the media, ma'am. Frankly, I wish you had come to me to talk about everything before you did this."

"I was told that you don't like the media, but I have to be frank here, Chief Mitchell. My life is on the line, and I don't much care what anyone likes right now. In the history of serial killers, the media has been shown to be a great help. I don't understand how you can push back so much research and risk the lives of so many by keeping the public in the dark."

He smiles at me, that kind of "fuck you" smile. The kind you give when you're forced to be polite. "We are actively researching this killer, and creating mass hysteria won't do anything but tie up my officers and keep them from finding this guy. My dispatchers are complaining that the phone won't stop ringing with bogus sightings and reports of what might have happened months ago. They can't get anything done. My entire department is out chasing ghosts generated by your statement Saturday. The media is in the front parking lot telling the world that we refused to make a statement and caused the death of all those women by not alerting the public to be diligent and pay attention."

"You did, sort of. Don't you think women might have paid a bit more attention if they knew? What if some of them might not have died? You can't be so obtuse as to think your way is right when it's been proven wrong with killers like Ted Bundy and The Boston Strangler, among others. We need to know."

"We tell women to pay attention, watch your drinks. Don't go home with strange men, all that. You don't listen. You still do what you want, and you get—" He stops himself, but I realize what he was about to say and take in a sharp breath. I need to be calm, but he's a moron. "Look." He breathes out, glancing at Doug, who sits with a frown on his face. "I think we need to back this up. I think you and I need to work together here, what do you say?"

"Work together?"

"Yes. I think you jumped the gun, but I'm sure we can fix this. Maybe instead of all this news, you can assist us in catching him."

I don't understand what he means, but apparently Doug does. He finally speaks up as he leans forward in his chair. "Wait a minute, are you thinking of using her as… as bait?"

Bait? "What? Is that what you mean?"

He looks around with shifty eyes and a weak smile. "Well, we can put you back in your apartment and set up cameras and wire taps. Watch the place. He'll come for you, and we'll be there to catch him. It's the fastest way. You want to save all these women, then this is the way to do it."

"What? Are you insane? You want to dangle me in front of a serial killer? You obviously don't know that much about this case if you think he'll kill me at my place. He'll take me, slash me to bits, and then rape some other woman in the mess. How can you risk my life like that?" I shout. I can't help it. This is TV movie shit.

"Come now, missy. We won't let that happen. You're the wife of one of our former officers. You'd have the entire department watching you. You see, when he comes for you—"

"No! *No!* Are you crazy? That's not how you catch a killer! That's how you catch people for identity theft or prostitution. You don't play with people's lives."

"Now, now, you need to calm down."

"Don't tell me to calm down!"

"Wren." Doug calls my name. I turn, seeing the warning in his eyes. I do need to calm down. This is the chief of police, not some redneck idiot. Maybe he's a bit of a misogynist, but surely he knows a bit of something, right?

I place my hand on my forehead and inhale. Exhale.

"I'm sorry. You're right. I do need to calm down. Look, Chief, you just don't know what I'm going through right now. I would like to do what I can to catch this man, but I can't die to do it. We can come up with something else, can't we?"

He nods. "Wren—can I call you that?" He continues before I can answer. "Look, I can make your probation go away. Or I can let it stand. We can work together, or we can work against each other. It's that simple. I'll tell you what, you think on that, and I'll be in touch soon, okay? I have to get this media dealt with." He stands, plants his hat on his head, and exits without pleasantries.

"He threatened you," Doug states once the door closes.

I nod. Indeed he did. "And he wants to use me as bait. Is he insane?"

"He's an entitled man with a lot of power, used to getting his way. Like a spoiled child, he'll find a way to throw a fit."

I sit down for the first time since entering his office, meeting his eyes across the desk. For a moment I wonder if he's thinking about me lying half naked with him, all tangled in that hotel room. I flush, realizing I'm thinking about it and we've been silent for too long.

"Let's go to lunch today, me and you," he says without moving his eyes from mine.

"I think I can manage that. I guess I should get back to work."

His smile warms me, calming me down a little.

I smile back before standing, then walk out without another word.

\* \* \*

When I turn the corner back into the room where my cubicle is, I see Lily's head pop up over one of her walls. Her eyebrows go up when she meets my eyes, and I'm followed back to my desk.

"How could you keep something like that a secret? What's it been, a month?" She grabs my guest chair, dragging it around to the back of the desk so she can better see me.

"Not exactly something people shout from the rooftops." I try not to glare at her or show my annoyance.

"You mean like talking about it on the news?"

I avoid her eyes, unsure of how to react. My initial feeling is indignation, even anger. How dare she question me? We aren't sisters, not even really friends. We hang out sometimes. That's it.

*Be nice.*

*But why? What if…?*

I turn to her, leaning back, crossing my arms. "It's not your business. I tell who I want to tell. I did what I did to save my life… save yours. All of yours." I raise my voice, sure someone is listening. Probably everyone. I imagine a dozen ears stretched to hear what might be the final speech of the dead woman so they can tell the story on some lame *Oprah* show or badly reenact it on *Dateline*.

"What if it was you? Sexually assaulted? Stalked? Do you really want to know what he did? What he's said? The pictures I've been sent?" I stand up. She pales, causing her red lips to stand out on her face, as if she's a prettily made-up corpse. "Get the hell out of here with your bullshit!"

She draws back, shocked, her blue eyes full of tears. I can practically see the arrow sticking out of her chest, barbed with my rough words. I almost regret it, but I can't take the time to have regrets, not now. Maybe later, if I live. If I survive.

"Wren, I just thought—"

"You have to understand something, Lily. I'm dying. Terminal. I may or may not pull through. I'm on the radar of a killer who is seven for seven. I'm number eight on whatever list he has. Me, not you. I've got a few weeks, maybe. It's entirely possible he won't wait; they say these killers get the itch and the murders get closer and closer together. But these sexual sadists are so methodical, I'm hoping this is what gives me time, forces him to bide his time and wait. Just leave me alone, okay?"

I find tears in my own eyes now. Maybe I said too much. Maybe I was mean, too rough. I want to apologize, but I don't. Instead, I sit down and open my drawer, grabbing a fast food napkin to dab my eyes. I offer her one, which she accepts.

"Sexual sadist?" she squeaks, barely a whisper.

I nod, not wanting to say any more, as if the knowledge will conjure him. The very idea makes me nauseous. The urge to gag almost becoming too much as I recall the blood… the body.

The woman. Now she has a name, a face. Number seven.

"Don't ask me, please. I can't."

I watch her rise, expecting her to storm out after telling me off. Instead she hugs me, pulling me in the way my mom used to, her chin on my head. "I'm so sorry, Wren. I understand now."

Does she? I doubt it, but I hug her back, forcing my tears to stop.

"Wren?" My phone. It's set to speaker for internal calls. It's the receptionist's voice, male, flamboyant, a sweet guy from our few chats. "Wren, there are media people here asking for you."

Media. They found me. I bet Chief Redneck sent them over here. Asshole.

I pull away, looking to Lily as if she might give me an answer. "Um, thanks," I toss out, and he hangs up. "Media, crap. What do I do?"

She shrugs. "I have no clue. Do you want to talk to them again?"

I shake my head. "No, there isn't anything else I want to say."

I don't know who else to call, so I call Doug. He tells me he'll get rid of them, but I know they'll probably just wait down on the street.

My phone rings, my personal phone.

"Hello?"

"Wren? This is Connie Beachem from Channel 54. I wanted to ask you a couple of follow-up questions about your probation and drunk driving—"

I hang up on her.

*Damn, what did I do?*

# CHAPTER SEVENTEEN
## WHAT WAS THAT NOISE?

*I HAD TO TURN MY PHONE OFF. IT WON'T* stop ringing. I can only hope they don't get my work cell; since I've only given it to a few people, it's less likely, but you never know with these vultures. I need to relax and find a way to get away, to forget and pretend this isn't happening.

I could get fucking drunk.

And that's what I decide to do.

The media is waiting, just like I expected. Doug sneaks me out in his SUV with darkly tinted windows and drives us to the liquor store. When we arrive, I'm still on the phone with Ricky, who's trying to talk me out of it because we work tomorrow.

"So what? My boss is here buying alcohol. He's not going to yell at me." I laugh, handing Doug a bottle of tequila. He grabs a bottle of Jack Daniel's and mixers.

"What do you want to drink?"

Ricky sighs into the phone. "What are you getting?"

A couple of hours later, we sit around the table with the cards out. Ricky is trying to tell us how to play Presidents and Assholes, a drinking game based on the card game VC, short for Viet Cong.

"This sounds hard." I take the cards he slides across the table.

"It's not that hard. We'll do a practice round." He winks at me.

Turns out it's not hard, but I'm just not very good at it. I'm pretty lit, and in that moment when everything is funny as hell, I hear the door and get up, almost falling down when I get tangled up with the legs of my chair.

"Don't," one of them calls out, though I don't know which.

"Please. Killers don't knock." I wave whoever off and open the door. "Well, fuck," I murmur as I stare right into eyes I never expected to see here.

"Hello to you too." Alex raises an eyebrow. Her long hair is pulled up into a perfect high ponytail. She's not dressed in work clothes but rather jeans, heels, and a blouse.

"What are you doing here?" I struggle not to sound drunk, sure that I'm failing miserably. "Oh, I forgot to check in again."

"You did. You keep forgetting that I'm worried about you, and I haven't checked on you since you moved in here. I needed to see your living situation, and I was in the area. I need to come in."

I swallow, glancing at the guys. She's not asking if she *can* come in—she *will* come in.

I'm screwed. Drunk. I'm not supposed to be drinking. But I'm not driving, right? I'm at home.

But this isn't my home. It's Ricky's home, not mine anymore. My home is an apartment with all my stuff in it that I haven't been able to sleep in for a while now. I want to go there, to my real home.

The reality hits me that since this started, this is the first time I've thought of that apartment as home.

"Okay then." I throw the door wide and make a grand gesture of bowing deep at the waist, almost falling over again. "Welcome to Ricky's house. Ricky, the guy who's hiding me from a killer, you know. Also, he's my estranged husband. Don't forget that part." I point to him.

He waves, drink in hand. "Hey there."

"This is Alex," I continue, "my probation officer, and I think we're friends. We are friends, right?" I slur, turning to her. "Are you arresting me? Maybe jail would be a great place to hide."

She smiles at Ricky and Doug, then sets her purse down. "Are you drunk?" She makes her way to the table, looking over the cards and the bottles. "And yes, I am your friend."

"Um, yes. To being drunk."

"But we're taking care of her." Doug stands. "I'm her boss and friend. She just needed a break, you know?

Stress relief."

Alex nods. "I totally understand. Well, you aren't driving anywhere, so I'd say you're in the clear. I won't tell. Can you show me around so I can write the report? I've needed to make this visit for days."

Ricky stands up, sober enough I suppose. "I'll do it. Wren, you sit." He pats the chair I was sitting in and then offers his elbow to Alex, who takes it with a smile. He leads her down the hall.

"She has to check where you live?" Doug whispers across the table.

"Yeah, I think she has to verify that I'm staying where I say I am, in case… you know. She checked my apartment too. She came during the day that time, but I guess she's been busy. She's always commenting about her caseload." I shrug, gathering the cards and trying to shuffle them. "She's been really great since all this started. She's been a friend to me."

"Makes sense. At least she cares. I'm sure that some fudge reports, say they visited when they didn't, all that stuff. It's bound to happen when you put so much work on people. How is she?"

"She's always nice, friendly. I've had no problems with her. At least she's not some power-crazy bitch." I laugh just as they walk back into the room.

"Nice place," Alex says.

"Thanks." Ricky smiles. "Want to play cards?"

She chews on her lip, seemingly debating internally.

"You're welcome to join us," I add. "We won't tell.

You only live once." I laugh, snorting at my own joke. "I ought to know."

I can tell by the looks exchanged that they don't know what to say, whether to laugh or not.

"Lord, it's a joke. Calm down." I roll my eyes, picking up my drink. I know I should take it easy—work is going to be a bitch tomorrow—but for now, I just don't have it in me to care.

"Well, if you insist." She smiles at me. "I assume you are insisting, right?"

I laugh, nodding. "Yes, totally. What can I get you?"

"Beer is fine."

And the evening wears on. I finally do switch to water, then whisper to Ricky that I have a wicked craving for pancakes, so he and Alex end up in the kitchen cooking. Drunk food is the best food there is, right? Fattening, rich, greasy.

Doug and I sit on the couch flipping through the Amazon Prime listings for something to watch, though I don't think either of us is really paying attention. I'm so buzzed I can barely get my eyes to focus without squinting.

"You can skip work tomorrow if you want to," he offers, cruising through British mysteries.

"Nah, I'll probably just be late. Thanks for hanging with me tonight."

He shrugs. "No problem. Glad I could do something for you. It's going to be okay. You do know that, don't you?"

Turning my head, I look over into alcohol-dulled eyes. He means it. Probably can't let himself think any other way. Some can't handle it.

Of course, I'm assuming. Maybe he's just that optimistic. Maybe he really does think so.

Everything will be all right.

I can't swallow it, like a pill that's too big to force down. Maybe I'm just too realistic. Maybe I'm being hostile. But I don't want to go down as this bitter, ugly, pissed-off woman. I want to be indignant. Righteously angry, shaking my fist and banging it on the podium. I want my obituary to say "She died fighting. She gave her all in hopes that it might stop him from killing again."

If they can't keep him from killing me, maybe they can be sure that I'm the last. That there isn't another.

It's the first time I've considered these types of thoughts. Perhaps the alcohol is making me brave.

I turn back to the TV and see Doug's put on a newly released movie.

"It might not be okay. I might die. You might have to replace me."

"I don't think so." He shakes his head, then peeks over his shoulder. He's checking to see where Ricky is. I can't help but smile when he leans over, his whisper in my ear sending a chill down my spine. "But I think it's just risky enough that you need to let me fuck you a few times."

I laugh, a girlish giggle. He chuckles, and I sneak a

look at him. He's close. He wants to kiss me but knows he can't.

I bite my lip and choose not to reply, not wanting to give anything away. I don't know if it would be cheating. "You're crazy," I finally say.

"You hesitated. And you didn't say no." He winks.

I laugh again before standing and walking off.

In the kitchen I find Alex laughing at something Ricky said while flipping pancakes. Ricky is pushing scrambled eggs out of a pan with a spoon.

"Is it ready?" I ask, taking in the scent. My mouth waters.

We eat, and soon the night ends and Alex and Doug go home. I tuck in on the couch, not trusting Ricky not to try anything since we're both drunk.

For the first time, I really don't want him to. Maybe it's the alcohol, maybe it's the possibility of the end of my life, but I don't feel like wasting any more time pining over him, regardless of the circumstances of his "mistake."

\*\*\*

The next morning, I wake up at eight and am struggling to shower away the hangover when I hear it.

A laugh.

It's deep and carries through the closed bathroom door, sounding like it's just a few steps down the hall. A man's laugh. In the bathroom just outside the shower curtain.

The dog isn't barking. *Where's Duke?*

I freeze, covered in foam, razor in hand. My heart either slows to an undetectable pace or races so fast I can't measure it. I stop breathing so I can hear any movement.

Maybe it's just Ricky.

I need to look, see if someone's there. I can't make my voice ask.

Maybe I imagined it. Maybe it wasn't real.

I strain to listen and hear nothing. Not a sound.

I start breathing again and step back under the hot water.

It's there again. A chuckle, rough and male. And not Ricky. This time it's in here with me, but I didn't even hear the door open. I didn't feel the cold rush of air you get when you open the bathroom door and let the steam out.

But I heard it. Someone is here. Someone opened that door.

*Oh God, he's come for me.*

*What the fuck do I do?*

My first instinct is to cry, but I force it back, knowing it won't help me. I look around for something I can use to protect myself but find only soap and shampoo. Won't help me unless I plan to wash him to death.

Where is my phone? I think hard, scrambling for an answer.

I left it in the bedroom.

I hear a door, distinct. Slamming, maybe the front

door judging from the direction it came from.

Did he leave?

This is where I die. I just know it.

Maybe a mad dash to the kitchen for a knife, maybe something heavy. I can't stay in here all day.

An idea hits me.

I reach out carefully without looking, grabbing and lifting the lid off the back of the toilet, almost dropping it. My hands are slick, and it's heavy, heavy enough to bash in a skull. I manage to hold on and clutch the cold porcelain to my naked body, steeling myself to pull back the curtain.

One.

Two.

Three.

*Ready or not, here I come.*

*God help me.*

The curtain in my hand, my heart beating like a conga drum, I open it. Naked, cold, and dripping wet, I don't reach for the towel yet, gripping the lid in both hands, ready to do what I must if someone is standing in the bathroom.

But no one is here.

I breathe out in a rush, feeling the tears start to threaten me yet again. Nothing is amiss, just how I left it. I put the weapon down long enough to wrap the towel around my body and then pick it back up. My hair drips down my back, giving me a chill.

Someone was here. I heard him laugh. I couldn't

have imagined it.

Where is the fucking dog? God, what if he killed him?

I've got to go out that door. Get my phone. Call someone.

I stare at the door, white and ominous before me. What if it's the only thing that's between me and him? Is he waiting? Hiding? Did he pretend to leave? Is he just fucking with me?

Oh God, I'm going to die. He found me again, and he's going to actually kill me.

I'll have to move. Leave here. At least try to get away, naked or not.

The doorknob is warm from the shower, wet and slick. I hear my heart beating, my blood rushing in my ears. It's loud, deafening, topped only by my breathing, which comes in short pants.

I put my ear to the door, silent, holding my breath. I hear nothing. Not a sound. I imagine him on the other side, smiling, amused with his ear pressed to the same door. Can he hear my heart beating? I lick sweat off my upper lip and rub my palms on the towel.

Closing my eyes, I breathe and count and then open them.

*Just do it.*

I turn the knob, opening the door a crack, a sliver through which to peek. Cool air invades the warm humidity of the bathroom, but there's nothing beyond, just the empty hallway.

Wider. Nothing.

Wider still, sticking my head out.

I don't see him, so I open the door wide enough to allow my body to pass through and step out, head turning on a swivel, eyes wide. Toilet lid in hand, I bolt down the hall like someone running up the basement steps, afraid of the monsters in their imagination. I make it to the bedroom, just a few strides away, and open the door.

Then I crumple to the floor.

# CHAPTER EIGHTEEN

## FOUND AND LOST

I'M SHAKING SO BAD I CAN'T STAND UP. Heaving sobs, scrambling like a crab heading backward out of the room, my weapon abandoned. I won't go for my phone. I can't.

There's blood everywhere.

It's like he took a bucket of it and threw it in the air. There's splashes on everything in the room— the bed, the floor, the walls. It stinks, metallic and rotten.

I search the room; my phone is on the nightstand. With fresh determination, I stand up. He's gone. This won't hurt me.

I enter the room, and the smell makes me wrinkle my nose. Pools of blood sinking into the carpet make me gag when I accidentally step in it barefooted. It's cold. Grabbing my phone, I rush back out. I see the front door wide open, gaping. I heard it slam; he must have done it to mess with me.

The dog is gone. I guess he just opened the door and let him out, then did whatever he wanted. Maybe he took him, killed him. I hope I never find out.

How did he even get in? How did he keep this blood from coagulating? Is it old? New? Human?

My first call is to Detective Small, who doesn't answer, so I call 911. I'm told not to touch anything by a monotone voice over the phone.

Then I call Doug and Ricky. I suddenly wish my mom was alive. She's been gone so long that I don't think of it much. But now I'd give anything to have her back for a minute, even a second of wisdom and comfort that only a mother can give.

It seems like a long time, but it's only minutes before the police arrive—a patrolman, followed by more, and then the detective shows up. I'm still in just a towel with three men surrounding me when Ricky arrives, eyes wide and totally freaked out.

"What happened?" he asks, even though I already told him.

I'm crying, sitting on the couch, clutching the towel for dear life. "Go look. And get me some damn clothes." I wave him toward the room.

"Stop. I'll get something." Small puts a hand on his shoulder. "Don't want you in there touching anything."

"Is it that bad?" Ricky is clearly itching to go see his bedroom, but he stays put as he's told.

"Pretty nasty. Don't know if it's human blood or not. We'll have to get it checked. We're going to be here for a while."

He glances at us, silently telling us to get out of here. Find a place for the night. Let them work without the hovering.

I want to be by myself. I haven't been alone since this started. I want to go home. Be in my own bed, my own apartment. I'm not sure if it's worth the risk, but I think asking Ricky to come stay at my house might be okay, for a night. I can't come back here knowing he found me.

"How could he find me?" I ask, wiping my eyes.

The patrol officer turns to me. Small has vanished down the hall. "It's easy to find people, way easier than anyone thinks. No one can hide anywhere for long these days. Takes drastic measures to really vanish." The officer is young, maybe early twenties. Looks green.

"I guess that's true. Everything is online now," I mutter, wondering what to do. How to hide in a world where no one can hide. Lose my name, change my hair, move to Mexico. Get lost in some resort working as a waitress, get a tan. Leave all this behind. It sounds amazing, really. Starting all over. Running away. Would he find me? Or would he give up and find someone else? A purely selfish move, but saving one's own life usually is.

Small comes back with clothes in his arms, handing them to me neatly folded.

"Thank you. I'm going to go change." I take the

clothes and head to the bathroom.

When I get back, Ricky and Small are huddled, and I discover that CSU is on the way to tear the room apart. Doug is standing in the doorway looking perplexed and out of place, not sure what to do with himself. I let the other two continue to share their secrets and bring him up to speed.

"You two can stay with me if you want," he offers.

I don't know about that. I tell him I'll have to see what Ricky wants to do, and he claims to understand.

God, I want to go home.

I feel like I'm losing myself in all this mess—who I was, who I am. Now all I am is running, hiding, crying, and freaking out. I want my life back. I want me back.

Wish in one hand… as they say.

"Let's just let them work," Ricky says, offering Doug his hand as an afterthought.

"I need to get to work, I guess." I sigh. "I want to go home."

I look up at Ricky and he nods, seeming to understand, but then he says, "I don't know if it's a good idea or not. The guy has been there a couple of times."

"It doesn't matter, does it? He found me here. He'll find me anywhere."

"I'll come stay with you, then, I guess," he mutters, glancing over his shoulder.

I feel like telling him I'm sorry, as if it's my fault. As if I did it by accident or something. It's ridiculous, so I don't. I just look from one man to the other, then down at my feet. "Let's get out of here. Doug, can you take me to work?"

He gapes at me, obviously baffled that I'd even offer to go in after this. But staying home and moping won't help, will it? Might as well get on with the short bit of life I have left.

"Sure thing."

# CHAPTER NINETEEN

## HOME AGAIN

BY THE TIME I GET TO WORK WITH DOUG, I've talked myself into it. It wasn't hard, just giving in really. I'm going home. If this person, this… beast can find me anywhere, then why hide?

I call him a person because I know he is, he must be, but it doesn't seem to fit. How can a person do this? And to call him a beast isn't really fair. Animals don't do that, killing for sexual pleasure. This lust that seems to push him, it really makes you think. When you consider all the forces that make a person, that hold them together and are that hidden, unseen force that drives them, the secret thought that pushes their decision one way or another, what's stronger than lust? Not much.

Lust isn't just sex, you know. It's an almost uncontrollable want. A desire that becomes an emotion, a taste on your tongue, a thought that won't go away.

An ache. It can be for anything, really. A lust for life. A lust for blood. A lust for pure, animal sex. He must be human—a man who has a hunger so powerful he can't stop himself.

I suppose lust is the strongest emotion, when you really think about it. We all feel it. Some are just better at denial, I suppose.

I ride with Doug up the elevator, feeling his eyes on me. I can almost hear the questions he isn't asking me, see the thoughts that hide behind his eyes. I don't speak or ask or even look directly at him. I've decided that I'll go home, back to my apartment, and I don't much care if anyone comes with me.

These men who've surrounded me will want to protect me, but I don't really think they can. I think Ricky acts in guilt, hoping to undo what was once done by protecting me, as if keeping me alive might alleviate his issues with Angela's death. And Doug, I'm not sure what he's doing, why he would glue himself to me, an almost sure lost cause. But here he is, watching me, offering his home to me, willing to stand up between me and this thing that's coming after me.

I think I'm numb. After this morning, I have to be to keep my sanity. If not for the numbness and the hollowness, I would run, screaming and crying like mad, out of this elevator and into the street.

I can't hide, I know, but I can stand up and pretend I'm ready for what's coming. I can throw myself into traffic and hope a bus hits me. I can sit and cry and beg him when he shows up to get his release. These are my options. I wonder what's worse, and then I answer my own question before I ask it. Worse than dying? Worse than meeting your end at the hands of a murderer? Knowing it's coming. Having foreknowledge. That's what's worse. Counting down the days like a fucked-up advent calendar.

As I sit at my desk, I text Ricky to tell him I'm going home tonight. We text back and forth all day, about the police, the investigation, the fact that I can't get to my stuff and neither can he until they release the room.

Was the blood human? Did he drain her and save it so he could use it to get off? Does it matter that it was cold? Ugh, the smell. I feel sick, bile rising in the back of my throat, and I reprimand myself for allowing such deviated thoughts into my mind. I shouldn't think such things. Shame on me. But that's what the blood is for, right? Is he angry that he had to use his stash to punish me?

What if that blood was all that was stopping him from killing me? Holding him back?

I've got to stop this. I stare at my computer, at an email, at my boss's calendar, but I don't really see anything. I need to focus and get to work. Stop all this and think about something easy. Be normal.

Tears burn my eyes. I won't be normal again, will I? Normal is long gone.

Music. Maybe that will distract me from my own mind. I put on music at a low volume, trying to focus, but I can't. I need to go home and find a way to clear my head.

I stand up and march down the hall to Doug's door, finding it open and him behind his desk, eyes on his computer. I enter, closing the door behind me, and then I burst into tears. He's on his feet in an instant, my outburst surprising me as much as it obviously does him.

"I can't concentrate. I can't turn it off. I can't find normal, or myself, or think about anything that isn't…." I shudder and sob, sitting down on the black-and-brown leather couch, grabbing a decorative throw pillow to hide behind.

I watch him turn and go to his hidden bar, making me a drink. I don't object, accepting it when it's offered; it's cold and damp, full of something clear over ice. It tastes like vodka and club soda, and I wince after taking a large sip of the strong mixture, hoping to fill my mouth with something besides the taste of bile.

Doug sits beside me, and his body language tells me that he doesn't know if he should touch me or say something.

"I don't know what to do anymore." I inhale a deep breath, trying to calm down. "What do I do?"

"I don't know." It's the first thing he's said since I walked in.

I want to feel alive, to forget. Pretend for a moment.

Acting on impulse, I lean over and kiss him, taking his lip between my teeth and invading his mouth until his groan tells me he wants more. There are still tears on my face when I pull my skirt up and straddle his lap, aching to feel his hardness between my legs, something to grind on and make me feel something besides afraid. His hands are in my hair, then up my shirt as my hips rock back and forth over the thing that presses firmly against his zipper and against me. I'm so grateful that he doesn't embarrass me by stopping me or reacting. He just goes with it, as if he knows it's what I need.

"Please." I whimper the word into his mouth, opening my eyes to see him watching me with a deep blue glaze. "Please." Then a thought. "Will anyone come in here?"

He shakes his head. "No."

I don't think. I can't. I'm dying anyway. Fuck it.

I reach down, and he groans when I open his pants, when I let him pull my panties aside and I slip down on top of him. His eyes roll back, his hands firm on my hips. I bite my lip and breathe heavily as I ride him, deep and slow, not crying anymore.

Fucking my boss on the couch in his office. I don't know if that's a high or a low. Good or bad.

I come fast and hard—breaking on him, bending forward, muffling my moans into his body, his hands in my hair. I feel his one deep, hard thrust, pushing himself deeper so he can come too. He grips me tight and grunts through clenched teeth. I watch his face as his eyes roll and close.

Then I smile, and so does he. I laugh, feeling okay

again—alive, sated, even relaxed.

He kisses me tenderly, softly. "You just fucked me," he whispers.

I nod. "I did. I don't even know what to say."

It occurs to me that I'm still sitting on him, with him inside me. I rise up and off him and wonder if I should ditch my now soaking wet panties. He tucks, zips, and grabs a wad of tissues from the box on the desk to make sure he doesn't have anything on his pants.

"I feel like I should say thanks." He laughs, then looks up. His eyes turn sad, probably because I'm teary again. "Hey, come here. Come here." I sit in his lap like a child, cuddled tightly, rocked while I cry softly. "Sweetheart, it's okay."

"No, it's not. I just had unprotected sex with my boss. I had a complete meltdown and screwed you to keep from losing my mind."

He laughs before kissing the top of my head. "Of all your problems, that's a small one, I think. And I've had a vasectomy, so don't worry."

"I don't think I'm going to get any work done today." I let his vasectomy go by without comment, grateful for one thing that's gone my way. I'm too upset to follow up with the normal curiosity of why a man his age got snipped.

"I can understand. You want to go home?"

"No." I really don't. "I just want to be normal again."

He holds me a little tighter, and it's comforting on

some level. Then I start to wonder if I'm supposed to tell Ricky that I screwed Doug today. Would it hurt him to know? Do I care if it would? I'm not a vengeful person, but I feel that I've leveled the playing field, and maybe looking at him won't hurt so much now.

"I'll take you on a trip, just me and you. We can run off and stay until this has all blown over." I think he's only half teasing. Maybe he would take me away.

I lift my head and look into his eyes. He's so very handsome with that just-fucked smile as he stares into my eyes.

"You probably would, wouldn't you? And when we got back, everyone would be whispering about us."

He laughs, and it makes me smile. I'm glad he's happy—obviously worried about me, but happy otherwise. "I would, and who cares about them?"

I shrug. I do on some level, but not really, not when it comes right down to it. "I guess that's true. All this is just so hard. I can't keep drinking and fucking my way to the end of this, you know?"

He nods. "But I'm here if you change your mind."

I giggle; I can't help it. It feels good to smile, to laugh. Maybe I'm being too serious, I don't know. But this is part of his game. It has to be. Fuck with them until they go nuts, and then end it once and for all. "If I live, I'm going to end up a drunken slut." I climb off his lap and sit on the edge of the sofa.

"No you won't. You're coping the best you can. So many people would just freak out or shut down. You're doing pretty well, I'd say."

"It's part of the game, huh?"

He nods. "I'm sure. He understands that knowing what's coming is messing with you.. Did any of the others know?"

I shrug. "I don't know. Maybe. Maybe they all just thought they were being stalked or something, but if he sent them pictures like he sends me, I can't imagine them thinking it was nothing. They would have figured it out, surely. Which also blows my mind since they never seemed to report it."

"Maybe they did. Maybe no one ever connected it."

I blink once, twice, then look at him. "What do you mean?"

"Maybe they were living somewhere else. Maybe they reported it as harassment and the cops never put two and two together. You never know. This chief, who knows what kind of reporting he's doing, what kind of investigation. I would think the FBI would have taken over once they caught wind of a serial killer."

"How could they be so stupid though? All they would do is run her name and see what she called in, right?"

"You're making a lot of assumptions. Let's get our hands on those police records and look for ourselves."

I bite my lip, thinking on what Doug said, the wheels in my head turning, grinding. It's something to work on, hold in my hands, something I can do besides wait. Dig on my own. "Is it that easy to get those records?"

"Yes. I'll go to the station on my way home tonight and do the request. Might take a few days, but I'll get my hands on them for you. We can take a look together."

"Okay, thanks." I meet his eyes, and suddenly I don't know what to say. He leans over and kisses me sweetly; I like the way he tastes. I lick it off my lips as he stands up, offering his hand to assist me to my feet. "I guess I'll go pretend to do some work." I laugh.

"All right. Try to relax, even just a little."

Nodding, I walk out. As I pass through the room back to my desk, I wonder if they can see it on me. The afterglow. Did they hear something?

I keep my head down and sit at my desk, assuming that, for now, they don't know anything.

\*\*\*

My apartment is stuffy. The AC hasn't been on, so it's hot and smells like stale air. Ricky walks in behind me, dropping his duffel bag by the door. Down the hall, I turn on the air; it clicks and comes to life, blowing fresher, cooler air into the space.

I've missed my apartment. It's small and nothing like the home we used to share, but it's mine. Home.

In this moment, I find a flicker of determination, the strength to say I won't let anyone run me out of my home again, out of my life. I'll stand strong, one way or another. Even if it's not true, it makes me feel better for a second.

I stand in the doorway of my bedroom with my hand on my forehead. The police left a mess, the crime scene unit taking their evidence and leaving me to clean up the aftermath. The mattress sits up against the wall with large sections cut out of it, chunks missing.

"Need a new mattress, I guess," Ricky comments, startling me. I didn't know he was behind me.

"I had been sleeping on the couch anyway. I can't—" I stop short of saying it out loud, that I don't have the money to buy a new mattress today. I don't want him to think I'm hinting around. I don't want anything from him.

"You can't what?"

"Nothing."

"Maybe it's not so bad. Let's see." I watch him step into the room, maneuver the thing back onto the bedframe. We both eyeball it. There are holes everywhere, with springs sticking up out of them. No one could sleep on this and not wake up with pain all over. "I guess I'll haul it to the dumpster for you." He laughs, a kind of snorting sound. "Do you want me to help you? I can go with you to pick something. I don't mind." He meets my eyes across the room.

I can't do it. I can't stand here and let him offer to help me get a bed, expecting to sleep beside me in it not knowing that I'm finished, or what I did… or that I might die. It's not fair, to him or Doug or me or anyone. I just don't have time to waste on this anymore. Whatever fear or doubt that I had only weeks ago seems to be gone. I suppose the threat of death, my final end, makes it seem like a silly thing to worry about. Realizing how short life really is, not knowing when the hammer might finally come down does that.

I have to tell him. He needs to know before it's too late, before he or I get hurt.

I swallow thickly, hesitating. The look on my face must give something away, because his smile fades, almost turning into a frown.

"What? What's wrong?"

If not for this terminal whatever this is hanging over me, I wouldn't be in this situation. I never would have dropped my panties for Doug, fucking him today. I wouldn't need a new bed. But here I am, in jeans and a sweatshirt, about to cry.

"I just want my life back," I mumble, not even meaning to say it out loud. He takes a step toward me, and I shake my head. "It's not fair to you," I toss out, backing up and turning away.

"I told you—"

"I slept with my boss." I say it with my back to him, without turning to see his face. I sense that he's stopped walking and only hear the soft hum of the air conditioner. "I… I…," I stammer but don't go further.

"You slept with that guy Doug?"

I nod. I mean to continue, but I never get the opportunity.

"Fuck." He's angry. "Fuck."

I hear footsteps, the movement of his body. I see

him walk around me, not bothering to look back. He crosses the room to the door and picks up his bag, then walks out.

# CHAPTER TWENTY

## GIRL TALK

I'M LEFT ALONE FOR THE FIRST TIME IN days, weeks maybe. I don't know if I should laugh or cry. At least that's how it seems. I went from always being alone to almost never, so the lack of company is acute.

I take a deep breath and release it. In the past, the weeks before, I'd come home and eat dinner, then watch my shows or read. I'd go for a run maybe or do some grocery shopping. Sometimes I'd hang out with Lily or go to dinner with a friend. My time was mine; I could do what I wanted.

My time isn't mine now. It belongs to him, the beast who's doing this to me. He owns me until this is over.

I should call Ricky, but I don't. I don't care if he's mad. He deserves to be angry, to feel bad after what he's put me through. I owed it to him. I need to tell Doug that I told him, but then he'll offer to come over and keep me company. He'd want to fool around, and I don't want to. I don't much want anyone touching me right now.

Maybe female companionship would work. But I was mean to Lily the other day, so I decide to turn to my other option.

I bite my lip and pull out my phone, texting Alex.

**Me: Hey, want to hang out? I moved back into my old apartment. You have the address.**

I pocket my phone, but then it pings again.

**Alex: Sure. When? Tonight?**

**Me: If you can. Need some girl talk.**

**Alex: Okay, I'll pick up Chinese and be there in a while.**

Maybe I should clean up. Do something besides think about men for once. Men who want to kill me, men who just want to fuck me, maybe even care about me. Let's not even talk about the L-word, not now. Not with all this going on.

Girls' night is just what I need. If not for what happened with Lily at work, I would invite her. I should anyway. Bury the hatchet, as they say. But I don't, and I don't even know why. Maybe I just don't want to deal with it, or maybe I just don't care about anything but myself. This has made me selfish. I don't think I was really a selfish person before, or was I? It seems like such a long time ago, normalcy. Remembering what I was before… this.

I turn on some music and start to clean up, lighting a candle to get the stale smell out of the place from lack of airflow. I'm standing in my bedroom doorway trying to think of what to do with the room when the knock sounds on the door. It must be her.

I turn my back on the room. I'll think about it later. The couch is good enough for me for now anyway.

After looking through the peephole—as if murderers knock—I throw open the door with a smile. She's standing there with a couple of white bags and a grin. Her dark hair is down and looks windblown. She's usually heavily made-up, expertly so, but not now. She looks almost bare faced, which gives me a strange sense of comfort knowing that I'm not the only one looking rough.

"I'm glad you finally decided to call me." She passes me, heading for the kitchen to set the bags on the counter. "Took you long enough."

"I know, I know." I stick my face into the bags, then grab plates.

"You got rid of your men for the night?" She raises an eyebrow at me, unpacking the food.

"Yes, I did. Which I should probably explain."

"Yes, you probably should. Surrounded by all that testosterone, woman, you must be exhausted." She laughs, loading up a plate with orange chicken and fried rice.

"No lie. But I have to confess, with all this stress and death chasing me, I did something bad."

We take our plates into the living room and sit on the couch.

"Bad or naughty?" She winks, biting an egg roll.

I flush, though I don't even know for sure why, then laugh, rolling my eyes at myself. It feels good to be light, even if it is a pretense, even if it's just for now. "Both, maybe." I regale her with the tale of Doug on the trip and then today in his office. She watches my face, eating slow forkfuls of takeout as she listens.

"He is sexy, really. Much older than you, right?"

I nod. "Yes, a lot. But I told Ricky today. I didn't know what else to do. I don't want to hurt anyone, and he's so determined. A woman he slept with was killed by this monster, and he feels guilty for her death, so I worry he's attached himself to me like it'll alleviate his pain or guilt or something. What if I do die? I don't want to hurt him, or anyone for that matter. I don't need him getting all attached to me only to have to bury me next month."

The words hurt to say out loud. Pinning a time on it like that, marking a calendar, is a sharp barb to the chest.

I look away from her, not wanting to see pity, emotion, or anything else that might be there. Eyes on my plate, I continue stuffing food into a stomach that's no longer hungry. "I know I'm probably being selfish, but—"

"It doesn't sound selfish to me."

I feel them coming. Tears blur my vision, spilling onto my cheeks. I blink, wiping them away, working hard to steady my voice. "I'm unraveling. I feel it, and I don't like it. Things like sex and drinking just make me feel alive, make me forget. I want my life back. I want to be in control."

"None of us is really in control. Anything can happen to anyone at any time. You just know, that's all. You know what might be coming. But the important question is"—she waves her fork at me—"how was the sex?"

I laugh, smiling at her. "Honestly? It was hot as hell." I feel my face grow warm again.

"Do you ever wonder if it's one of them?"

I shake my head. "No, it couldn't be. They say this killer gets off at the sight of blood, that it's maybe the only way he can. It can't be them."

Her smile fades. Can't blame her for that. "Really?"

"Yes, that's what they think. Said that's why he…."
I fade out, not sure I can go on.

"What?"

"It's disturbing."

"So?"

I take in a deep breath, blowing it out slowly. "It's why he kills and then rapes the new victim there, in the mess, with the body right there. It gets him off. The death, the blood. The power."

Her eyebrows go up, and then she looks down for

a moment, as if considering her food. Maybe it put her off. I regret saying anything, letting her talk me into telling her about it, but then after pushing the food around with her fork for a moment, she shakes her head. "That's really scary, sick. How can someone make sex such a dark, twisted thing?"

"People do it all the time."

"I know, and I don't get it. I get how it can just be easy, carefree, and not really mean anything. Just two people into a moment. But that dark stuff... I don't know."

"Everyone probably has some twisted secret thing they're scared to tell anyone. I guess it just gets the better of some people. I suppose I never wanted anything so much that it took over who I was, controlled me, became my entire existence."

"Doesn't that sound sexy though?"

I look up at her, surprised. "Sexy?"

"Yeah. The lust. It consumes you. To want something or someone so bad you can taste it. To throw caution to the wind and just give in to it because it permeates everything. It's erotic."

I don't know what to say. I watch her eyes, which are locked on me. Then she shrugs, setting her plate on the coffee table. "Never?"

"I mean, I have been turned on, but not—"

"Not the same."

"So you have had that?"

She gives me a slow nod. "Yes, I have."

Silence falls. I don't know how to respond. She makes it sound sexy.

She tilts her head. "Never had the hunger, huh?"

I shake my head, suddenly feeling left out, as if I've missed out on something. "No, I suppose not."

"Well, you're young, I'm sure you will. I am older than you are, after all."

"How old are you?"

She gives me a small smile. "Thirty-eight."

"Where are you from?"

She crosses her legs, forking a chunk of chicken. "I was born in Ecuador. My parents left and came to America when I was a baby, which is why I don't have an accent. My mother was adamant that I become a citizen as soon as I could. She would tutor me every weekend, and as soon as I turned eighteen, I became official. I worked in my parents' bail bond business from when I was sixteen. I didn't even go to college until I was a lot older."

"I didn't go at all. Never could quite get there." I shrug. "I met Ricky when I was nineteen anyway. He was twenty-five and had already graduated and had a good job."

"So he's six years older, right?"

I nod. "Yeah, he's thirty-two now."

"How did you meet him?"

"Blind date. My roommate at the time introduced us. I ended up in bed with him that first night." I laugh at myself. "We just clicked, I guess."

"It happens." She nods. "I graduated and didn't want to be a police officer, but I knew I wanted to help people somehow and be in law enforcement. Probation officer seemed okay, helping people turn their lives around. I started in the juvenile sector, but the kids are so difficult to deal with. I prefer adults."

"I can imagine. Hoping to help some kid who just doesn't want any help."

"Yes, they think they know everything. Kids are a calling, and I didn't have it in me."

"Understandable."

"Did you two want kids?"

"Eventually. I guess most everyone does, but we were enjoying our time together. I thought we were, anyway. He was enjoying more than I thought he was." I roll my eyes, waving my fork.

"What an ass."

"You can say that again."

"Are you going to divorce him? He seems to want you back."

I frown. "I don't care what he wants. He had me. He gambled; he lost." I don't answer the question, though I'm not sure why. I leave it open with the answer implied but not confirmed, shoving a forkful of food into my face instead.

When we're finished, I stand up and clear the plates, then toss her the remote. "Pick a chick flick or something."

She catches it, careful of her well-manicured, long

nails, and I take the plates into the kitchen, stuffing the leftovers into the fridge. There isn't much else in there. I need to go shopping.

"I have wine. Want some?" I call out, seeing a cold bottle of sweet red I bought weeks ago.

"Always." She laughs.

I grab the bottle and a couple of plastic glasses and sit beside her on the couch. She starts a romantic comedy, then pours us each a glass.

"To lust." She winks at me.

I snicker, clinking my glass against hers. "What the hell."

Hours later, we've watched movies and had more than the one bottle that I put out. It's getting late, and I worry about her driving home. She's pretty tipsy. As am I.

I stand in the hall in just an oversized nightshirt, having changed an hour ago. "You can't drive like this," I say.

"Where am I going to sleep, on that fucked-up bed?" She laughs.

"I have no idea. I sleep on the couch."

"It's not big enough to share."

"I know."

"You offer me a place to stay with no bed." She cocks an eyebrow at me. "I'll sleep in the tub."

We both start to laugh. "You take the couch; I'll sleep in the chair. It lays back. I'll be fine. I sleep like the dead."

She busts out into drunken giggles. "Fine. Can I have some shorts or something?"

I nod. "Yeah, I'll find something."

Before I turn, she grabs my arm. I stop, thinking she's going to ask me for something else, but instead I'm startled by a kiss. She moves in so fast that I don't see it coming, can't react and pull back. Her hand moves from my arm to my face, holding me in place as soft, plump lips that taste like wine and Chapstick press against mine. I can't even think, can't process what's happening to me.

Suddenly my mouth is open and my tongue is tangled with hers. She sighs and presses her body to mine, her breasts against my chest. She kisses me like she wants me.

I'm confused. I've never kissed a woman before, ever. I'm a little drunk, and honestly, it's not unpleasant. I almost like it.

The kiss goes on until I feel her hands on my thighs, tugging at my nightshirt. Then I pull back.

"What?" she asks in a whisper, her glazed eyes staring into mine. "Have you ever tried it?"

What do I say? "No thanks, I'm strictly into dicks"? I have no clue.

"Tried what?"

She flashes a smile. "Sex with a woman."

My head spins. Is it a curiosity? Is it on my bucket list? See if I can get off with a chick? My mind won't work. "No, I never have."

"We can try, play around, if you want to. I won't tell anyone." She lifts my nightshirt and peeks down at my soft pink cotton panties. "You know, get out of these for an hour or so."

"Alex—"

She kisses me again, tugging on my panties, trying to get them off my hips. I pull back, my heart racing, frankly shocked and getting a little upset. "Hey, cut it out." I push her hands off me.

"I have, you know. I've been with a woman. It's okay. I mean, I know it's your first time, so we could go slow and everything. It's just sex. Doesn't have to mean anything."

I suddenly want her to leave. I want to be alone. I don't want anyone bothering me or touching me. What is wrong with everyone? How did I go so long on my own, and now everywhere I turn, everyone wants to pull my pants down?

"I just want to be friends," I finally croak out, my voice hoarse and cracking. "Isn't that okay?"

She backs off, nodding. "Sure, sure. Of course. I didn't mean to make you uncomfortable, you know. Just…." She shrugs. "Sorry." She blushes, pink rising to her cheeks. She looks down and away, as if embarrassed.

Suddenly I'm sorry. Making a pass at someone and being rejected, someone who confused the issue by kissing back, not jerking immediately away and saying no, has to be difficult. "Hey, it's no big deal. Just two drunk girls, right?" I laugh it off.

She nods, flashing a smile that doesn't touch her eyes.

"I'll get your clothes and some blankets and stuff."

Not much else is said, and we tuck in quietly. I have to say, after today, I'm starting to understand what nuns see in convents.

# CHAPTER TWENTY-ONE

## DECISIONS

THE NEXT MORNING, I WAKE EARLIER than she does. She's asleep, curled up under a blanket, snoring lightly. Even after the weirdness, I'm glad for the company.

I put on a pot of coffee and then jump in the shower. I need to check my messages, my emails, all the things the media stirred up. Doug promised to get a copy of the evidence so we could do some digging. I want the names of the last victims. I want to see their faces.

It's only a matter of time before those faces are paraded on the news, image after image. A somber reporter, all the hoopla that follows. Doug said I should keep the chief on his toes, keep doing interviews. Force his hand. Pissing him off might work either way, but I have nothing to lose now.

I dress in leggings and a long tunic-style sweater. Alex is in the shower when I pass the bathroom. I make coffee and then sit down with my email and start to sort through it. I have an offer from the local news for an interview, a few from some papers and magazines, and a couple of others. As I stand in the kitchen, looking into the pantry for something to eat and thinking about getting groceries, a sad thought comes into my brain.

Do I make a will? Do I work out my wishes for my remains? I swallow hard. What does someone do when they know they might die? They prepare. They prepare those around them, and they live their last days.

I frown. Fuck that. I fight. I fight until I have no fight left in me.

"Morning." Her voice draws my eye. She stands in the kitchen, rolling her damp hair into a bun. "Hey, I'm sorry about—"

I shake my head. "Nah, don't be. We were drunk." I shrug. "I kissed you back. It's nothing."

She nods, still looking sheepish. "You sure?"

I smile, closing the pantry door. It's empty anyway. "Sure. Don't think anything of it. Wanna go eat? I have no food."

"Sure."

We go have breakfast, and she takes off after dropping me at the grocery store. Maybe a boring Saturday is just what I need. A day with no crazy, nothing but mundane. A day to myself. After I get the groceries home, I decide to go ahead and get a new mattress too. I go to the mattress store and finance a new queen-size bed, and I also get new sheets and a comforter. The police took half of what I had anyway, and maybe new, clean, untainted linen will help me sleep in my own bed again.

With same-day delivery, that night I stand in my bedroom looking at my freshly made bed. All I can see is blood though. The phantom red splashes. Imaginings of him standing over my unconscious body taking pictures. Of him dragging a dead woman out of my apartment, maybe over his shoulder as if she's simply drunk.

I swallow, turning, shutting the door. I tuck in on the couch once again, turning off my phone and settling in for a night in front of Netflix.

Pretend all is well.

\* \* \*

It's late when I snap awake to the sound of pounding on my front door. I guess I fell asleep. The room is dark except for the glow coming from the TV, which is now an old rerun of a black-and-white western. I yawn, grab my phone to check the time, and see that it's off.

Through the peephole, I see Ricky. He's the one pounding on the door. I unlock the latch and open it.

"Why don't you answer your damn phone?" he growls at me, coming inside without an invitation.

"I turned it off. I needed a break. Then I fell asleep." I shut the door. "I didn't mean to scare you. I'm sorry."

I turn on my phone, and after a minute I see all the missed calls and texts. It's nearly eleven.

Ricky sits heavily, looking both pissed and relieved

at the same time.

"I was afraid…." He shakes his head, looking away. "Anyway, I'm glad you're okay."

"Me too." I snort. "I had some drinks with Alex last night. She stayed over, and we had breakfast this morning. I just had a day to myself." I sit back down on the couch, under the blanket. Even with the new bed, I don't want to sleep in there alone. And I sure as hell am not going to invite him.

"I was hoping we might talk."

I swallow. I suppose I can't run from it forever, can I? Time to face some things, I guess, get it all out now that the playing field is semi even. "Okay, I guess we can try."

He takes a deep breath. "I know it's probably stupid to tell you that I'm sorry, but I am. What happened with Angela, it was a huge mistake. I wasn't thinking, I didn't plan it, and I never planned on it happening again. I will regret it for the rest of my life, and I will never forgive myself for doing it or for hurting you. I don't want a divorce, Wren."

I'm surprised when his voice breaks, tears swimming in his eyes. He didn't cry when I walked out. He did try to stop me, but he wasn't broken over it, not like this. I feel barbs in my chest, never having seen him tear up before.

"And this whole serial killer thing," he continues, "it's got everything so messed up. I know you'll come out of this. You will. You have to. I can't—" He shakes his head, blinks, and wipes his eyes. "I don't even care that you slept with Doug. I deserve that. We're separated, and you're scared. I get it. I just want… I want us. I want you. I chose you, and I always will."

"You're asking me for another chance?" I whisper. The words won't come out any louder than that. He wants me to come home. Be his wife again. I ache to say yes, but how can I? Knowing what he did? One stupid woman got to him so simply. So easily. All she did was ask and he was inside her in a minute. I can't. It was too easy. "How can you think that what you did is that easily forgiven when it was so easy for you to do it? There was no struggle. You didn't fight it and fall in love over time or something. She showed you her pussy, and you dove right in."

He blinks at me, ready to open his mouth and argue. I hold up a hand. "Stop. You know it's true."

"We've been married for six years. You are really ready to end that?" His voice cracks. "To start all over? Say 'never again'? I'm not ready to do that."

The emotion in his eyes breaks my heart, but what he did hurts more. "You were ready to end that when you unzipped your pants. You were my first everything. I married you as soon as I turned twenty-one. I can't ever forget how easy it was for you. Now that I know, I would never trust you again. I would always think you're going to do it again, and you would, especially if I let it go. It hurts, a lot, but you made this decision, Ricky. You did, all by yourself. You threw me away." I don't yell. I don't even raise my voice. The words are sharp enough on their own.

I pull the covers up, trying to be strong. I wish on some level that I was stupid enough to be weak, to let him back in. It would be easier, feel good for a while. However, I know it would be fleeting, and in the end I would hate myself for it.

"You want a divorce?"

"I don't want one, but we have to get one. It's over." The words hurt, so much. The end of such a huge part of my life. My love at nineteen. My first—I was a virgin.

The happy memories flooding in make me wonder if I'm doing the right thing. I let myself cry, watching him stare at me without speaking.

Then I see her face. Standing on my porch, her words, his face.

\* \* \*

It takes me a minute to understand what she's telling me. I frown, asking her to repeat it. She glances around, then looks at me and seems to steel herself. "I'm pregnant. Your husband got me pregnant."

I blink slowly as the words sink in. "My husband? You mean Ricky Addison?"

"Yes. I've been trying to reach him to tell him about the baby."

"Who are you?" My blood starts to rush; I can almost hear it in my ears. "When did this happen?" My face feels both cold and hot at the same time.

"A couple of months ago. I work in the records office at the police station with him. Look, I'm sorry to do this, but he's ignoring my calls. He won't talk to me. I've been trying to reach him, and he won't call me back."

And just like that, my world is black. Undone. The man I married betrayed me. Surely not. Maybe she's lying. But why would she lie?

Before I open my mouth, I see Ricky's truck. Matte black wheels throw gravel as he pulls into the driveway too fast. He always does. Through the tinted windshield, I barely see his face, the recognition when he sets eyes on her and me together, but it's enough. He gets out as if in slow motion, the color draining from his face, a mouthed "I'm sorry."

So he did cheat on me.

I feel dizzy, then angry. Real angry. I watch him with pissed-off tears in my eyes as he marches up the steps and turns her roughly with a hand on her arm. Her whole face lights up.

Shit, she's in love with him. It's all over her face.

"What are you doing?" His words are harsh. He glances at me and then back to her.

She heaves out a couple of breaths, touching his chest. He backs away, again looking at me. "You wouldn't answer me when I called. I didn't know—"

"Get the fuck out of here."

She blinks as if stunned. "But, Ricky…." She grabs

his arms and tilts her face up as if to offer her lips to him. "Ricky, I'm pregnant."

I feel sick, stunned to silence watching the display. My husband pales, and he's rough with her, cruel almost, as if it might ease my pain, make what he did less of a horror.

"Go. I told you it was a mistake. Fuck, how could you do this to me? This is my whole life." He glances at me, fear dancing in those eyes I love. Eyes she loves too. "You're a liar. Go home. Don't come back."

She looks between us, mouth agape, then flushes, suddenly embarrassed. Ricky turns, pacing, hands in his hair as he mutters swears. I stand mute, my whole world paused in this horrible moment.

She walks off crying, getting into her car and driving away. I watch Ricky pace for a moment, unsure of what to say or do. But then words just start to come out of my mouth. "It's true?"

He stops walking, his steps heavy. When he turns, he's pale, his eyes afraid. "I don't know what she told you."

I laugh until it turns into tears. "She said you got her pregnant, that you won't answer her calls since you had sex with her." The words taste bad in my mouth. Images of his hips pumping against hers, her begging for more, make me want to vomit.

"I... she... fuck. She's crazy. Wren—"

I turn, knowing him too well. He won't come out and say it. Can't really blame him. But his admission is there, between the lines.

I go inside, run up the hall, and pull out my suitcases, the ones we took on our honeymoon. I throw my things inside in a rush, trying not to think. This is goodbye. What's the point? Why allow him time to talk me out of this? We can't come back from it, so I'm leaving my life behind, my dream house, my love.

God, I loved him. Love—I love him. And fuck him for doing this.

\*\*\*

Will it ever not hurt? I suppose it will. I've been without him all this time, and I've managed. I wipe my eyes as he leans forward, elbows on his knees. "Maybe we can get some help."

"No. When this ends, if I live, I'll file for divorce. If I die?" I shrug. "I suppose you can be a widower. But this"—I wave my hand between us—"is dead. Remember how you feel right now, never forget it, because you did this all by yourself."

I cry as he covers his face; he's crying too. Not knowing what to say, I just turn my face away. I suppose this day was coming, and I'm not really sure what made me strong enough to finally face it. Maybe it's realizing that life really is short and wasting it is just… you just can't get that back. So pointless. I'm young. If I survive, I'll be okay.

"Wren, is there anything I can do? Can't you just

think about it?"

"I have, for months now. No one is sorrier than I am, Ricky."

I'm not sure how, but I watch him stand up. He tells me goodbye, gives me a long look, and then walks out the door.

I lock it, then sit down and cry myself to sleep.

# CHAPTER TWENTY-TWO

## NUMBER EIGHT

*I KNOW BETTER, I REALLY DO, BUT AT* this point, my give a damn is broken. By midday Sunday, I've told both Lily and Alex—tearfully, mind you—that I told Ricky I want a divorce. Together, they decided that I needed to celebrate my decision, and they were going to help me drown my sorrows. I mentioned Lily to Alex, and she told me in no uncertain terms that we would get together and demanded her number. I told her that I'd just had a girls' night Friday, and she laughed and said it didn't count. Then I think, *Three weeks*, and say fuck it.

That's what friends are for, she chimed. Lily agreed. They managed to convince me, and I even called Doug. We talked for a while, and he told me to take Monday off, promising me dinner Monday evening.

I've been a bit sad, the finality of everything making me wonder if I made the right decision. At the bar, when I tell the girls this, they lay into me, of course.

"Wren, don't. Once a cheater, always a cheater."

"If you take him back, he won't ever respect you, and he will do it again."

"You're right, it was way too easy for him to cheat. You're doing the right thing."

They give me practically every cliché in the book.

"You guys, I've been drinking way too much lately." I sigh when the waitress brings us a new round of drinks. "But hell, I've got a timer on my life, so who cares?" I down the fruity shot, knowing it won't be long before I feel it. I'm already buzzing. "This won't solve anything," I add, setting the glass on the table.

"It won't, you're right, but you can forget for a while, right?"

"Forget what? Let's see. That I'm probably going to be dead soon, that my husband sucks, that I'm about to be single, and that I screwed Doug." I tick them off on my fingers.

Lily's eyes widen, and I realize my slip. "What? You did what?"

I flush, biting my lip. Crap. "Um… nothing?"

She laughs, leaning forward. "No, no, no. You fucked him? When?"

I shake my head.

"Come on, you have to give me some details."

"No, I don't. You'll tell everyone." I don't know if it's the alcohol, but I feel embarrassed. Not that I gave myself to him but that she had him first, even if it was a mistake. I don't like it. It leaves a bad taste in my mouth. I don't want to compare, and I don't want her to either. I'm not jealous; it's just weird.

She frowns, furrowing her brow. "I won't tell anyone. But are you two a thing now?"

I shrug. "I don't know. I was freaked out that day, and it just happened. He's really pretty sweet."

"I didn't know you liked older guys." Lily smiles.

"Neither did I." I laugh, then flag the waitress down for a pitcher of beer. "But I guess I do."

Silence falls for a moment. I think Alex picks up on something, judging by the way she glances between us. "So, Lily, what's your story? Tell me about you."

Lily stirs her drink with her straw. "Me? Not much to tell."

"Oh, come on, everyone has something."

"Well, I graduated high school at sixteen. I went to college early, studied, discovered dick." She snorts, laughing at herself. "I graduated with honors. I know I could have done more, but eh." She shrugs. "So I'm a twenty-four-year-old paralegal. I do okay. I'm happy with it. It's easy, low stress for me."

I had no idea she was so smart.

"And you? You ever marry?" Lily asks.

Alex shakes her head. "No. Never met the right guy, I guess. I kind of got a late start. Worked my ass off for my parents for years. I got to college late."

"And here I sit, married, almost divorced, and the group idiot." I laugh. "Here's to us."

The girls laugh uncomfortably at first, but they raise their glasses and we all down our drinks.

"Let's go dance," I suggest. "This heavy shit is too much."

"I second that." Lily jumps up so fast that she knocks her chair over.

"Watch it, girl." Alex picks it up, giggling. And just like that, the heavy mood is gone and we forget.

The evening goes on, and we drink and dance late into the night. We end up closing down the bar. We all met at my apartment, and Alex is the only one who's sober enough to drive, so she drives us home.

"You guys can just stay the night. I got a new bed," I announce, smiling.

"Can we all fit?" Alex asks, turning into my complex.

"No, I don't think so."

"I call shotgun." Lily busts out laughing.

I giggle. "Is there shotgun for a bed?"

"I don't know, but I call dibs."

Alex is laughing as she parks. "It's fine, you two can stay here. I think I'm okay to drive home."

"You sure?" I ask.

"Yes, I'm fine. You two get some rest."

We say our good nights, and I lock the door behind her.

Lily stumbles down the hall, trying to get out of her jeans. I make sure all the doors are locked and alarmed, and then I crawl into bed beside her, sleep finding me in minutes.

\*\*\*

I wake up with a gasp, though I don't know why. Maybe I was dreaming. It's dark. I hear the patter of rain outside and distant thunder. My eyes won't focus.

I lie back, feeling Lily's body beside me, sticky, cool to the touch. No, cold. She's cold. It's past the point of skin that's chilled from sleeping without a blanket in a chilly room. This is something more.

I prod her and say her name. My heart starts to beat in a strange rhythm, thumping and skipping as I stand up, only just then realizing I'm naked.

My hand trembles when I reach for the light, only steps away. Hesitating, I hover above it, afraid of the light. I don't know why I'm afraid. She's just chilled, I tell myself. Just a hard sleeper.

I close my eyes and say a short prayer, hoping, begging it's anything else. It can't be, not really. Maybe I'm dreaming, and after I flick on the light, I'll wake up screaming and she'll be there beside me, frowning because I woke her up.

But there is a killer after me.

I swallow the saliva pooled in my mouth, then gag, forcing a deep breath to calm my stomach and my throat. Only then do I turn on the light.

The scream that comes out of me is otherworldly. It hurts my throat and makes me dizzy. I'm shaking so bad I can barely stand up.

He came back.

Lily is dead.

I've been sexually assaulted—I feel it in my thighs, the bruises. Looking down, I see the finger marks where he gripped my hips, the fresh bite. The blood.

Oh God, the blood.

But I can't tear my eyes from her. She's blue-gray and waxy. Her eyes are open and frozen in blank, empty horror. She's covered in slash marks, her throat gaping. I stumble from the room, hitting the wall in the hallway in a rush to get out, to unsee it all. There's a knock on the door followed by Alex's singsong voice calling a good morning to us. I unlock the door in a daze, and she walks in to find me standing bloody and naked, crying, panting, trembling.

Her eyes go wide, and she drops the bags of food she was holding. "What the fuck?" Her voice is strange, but maybe that's just to my ears. I feel odd, faint. Maybe I can't quite hear her. "Wren, what the fuck happened?"

When she shakes me, I realize she's moved and is in my face, hands tight on my forearms. "Talk to me. Are you hurt? Where's Lily?"

I blink. "Dead. She's dead." I cough out the words. "He assaulted me again. He was here." I can't make my mouth say rape or sexually assaulted, even after all this. I don't want to verbalize what I already know to be the truth, as if it's some sort of secret security blanket, a Band-Aid over my emotions that protects my mind from reality.

She steps away from me as if I've burned her. "He, who? The killer? That SMS guy?"

I nod. "I guess so. I suppose no one was screaming, since nobody came to check. We were drunk. Must have drugged us again." I sit down, unable to stand any longer. I wonder if my words are just ramblings or if I even make sense.

She gapes at me, horrified, pale, tearful. She picks up the blanket on the couch and wraps it around my shoulders before walking down the hall. I hear her gasp, followed by several swears, and then she comes back with tears on her cheeks. "Oh God. Did you call the police?"

"Not yet."

She dials 911. Soon enough, the place is crawling with cops. Detective Small is in my face, asking me questions, but they say I'm in shock, so I'm put into an ambulance and carted off. At the hospital, someone shows up and I'm treated as evidence. They collect samples from the blood all over me: my hair, under my nails, swabs from my genitals, anus. Only afterward am I allowed to shower, then dress in a hospital gown, told to rest and that someone will be with me shortly. I'm hooked up to an IV while I stare at a TV playing a rerun of *Everybody Loves Raymond*, but all I can see is Lily's empty dead eyes. All I can feel is the cold of her skin when I touched her.

As the fluids pump into my veins, I wonder what happened. Lily wasn't on his radar. This is out of his norm. Alex might be dead too if she had stayed. Why was I left alive?

I don't have my phone; I left with nothing, naked but for the blanket on my back. I'm glad no one is here. I know the police won't let anyone talk to me before they can, and the time alone is a blessing. But then I start to cry, and I curl up into a ball because I know I'm going to die.

He will find me, and he will kill me.

# CHAPTER TWENTY-THREE

## POLICE

IT'S LATE IN THE EVENING BEFORE Small walks into my hospital room. I'm half asleep. He looks tired, worn thin. He nods at me as I sit up, careful of my IV, and then he sits down and pulls a recorder out and a note pad.

"What happens now?" I say as he flips through his notes.

"I'm not sure. I've had an officer here on you all day long. I worry about letting you out of protective custody at this point."

I lay my head on the pillow, considering the idea.

He seems to find what he was looking for, saying, "I rushed all the labs from today, but that doesn't mean anything. They still do what they want. But I'm here because I need your statement. Tell me everything."

I relay what I know. The evening before, the drinking, coming home, locking the door. Everything, yet nothing. I have no memory of anything, just as before. He records me and scribbles notes.

"I don't know what else to say. I'm sorry it isn't much."

He shakes his head and looks up at me with tired eyes. "No, it's plenty. I think you must have pissed him off somehow. I don't know. He's never done this before. Or maybe he broke in to kill you and Lily was there, so he just figured he'd have one extra."

He says it so casually, but the words ring in my ears.

He came to kill me.

I would be dead if Lily had not been there.

Silent tears roll off my cheeks. No sobs, no moaning whimpers, just water on my face. I know if by some off chance I survive, I'll never be the same. I'll need help. I see the nightmares and flashbacks in my future. The permanent fear of the color red, screaming at the sight of blood.

"Will you allow us to take you into police protection?"

I pull back from the nightmarish daydream and look over at him. "Yes."

"I need to make some calls. Can I get you anything? Reach out to anyone for you?"

I stare straight ahead, feeling empty, blank. The trauma has snapped something, broken something inside me, I fear. "I don't know what to do anymore. My friend was killed because she was with me. Maybe keeping everyone away for now is a better idea." The words tumble out without thought. I hear them come out of my mouth, but I'm so disconnected, it's as if someone else said them. Maybe I need help. Maybe I'm losing it.

Crazy or dead. Great choice.

I watch Small step out after pocketing the recorder. He pulls out his phone, the door shutting behind him. I haven't called anyone since I got here. Alex is the only one who knows. Doug and Ricky will be worried. I should tell them I'm okay.

The detective walks back in and yawns, only to apologize to me for his fatigue. "Wren, someone will be taking you to a secure location when you're released tomorrow. We need to talk about who you tell and who you don't. I know Ricky would worry, and your friends, considering the situation, but I think it's best that no one knows where you are, only that you're safe."

I nod. "I don't even have my phone. I left it behind at the apartment. Is it evidence?"

"I'm not sure. I'll check. I can get you another one, if you like."

"I can wait until we know if they took it."

"Okay. I'll check on you in the morning. Get some rest."

I nod, wondering if I will sleep without dreaming. Hoping.

\*\*\*

When I wake the next morning, the room is silent. I

assume I'm alone, but when I roll over and open my eyes, I find that I'm not. Doug is in my room, pacing and looking down at his phone. The sound of me moving on the hospital sheets is loud in the quiet, drawing his eyes.

"Hey!" He pockets the phone and rushes to my side. "I heard what happened. I wish you'd called me."

His hands are on me, touching my hair and my hand, as if he can't believe I'm real. The warmth of his touch is comforting to me, makes me feel less robotic and crazy, more human.

I don't know what to say. I turn my face into his hand, pressing my mouth to his open palm, closing my eyes. He takes my face in his hands, his fingers in my hair, eyes gazing deeply into mine. "You aren't okay, are you?"

I shake my head. "Might not ever be okay again."

"You will be, someday. When it's over."

"You shouldn't be with me. Don't get killed for me."

He smiles, a sad laugh bubbling out of him. "I can't stay away. I worry when I don't hear from you."

"I know. I told Ricky I want a divorce; did I tell you?" Such a huge thing to forget, but my brain isn't working properly.

"No, you didn't. How did he take it?" Doug sits on my bed and pulls me into his arms. I feel the heat from his body, strong arms tight around me.

I close my eyes at the memory. "He cried. Asked me

to come home. I said no. I was upset, but—"

"I can't imagine." He caresses my cheek. "A person can only take so much at once. I'm concerned for your mental status."

I push my face into his chest, taking in the smell of his body. "Me too. Smart man. The detective told me that the killer might have come to take me last night, but when he found that I wasn't alone, he changed his plan."

He doesn't answer, and I don't blame him. His arms get tighter, his face in my hair on the top of my head. I listen to his breathing, wondering what to say to him now. Do I make plans? Cremation or burial? I have nothing to leave behind. Ricky would get whatever I do own, so I don't need a will. I'm young and haven't much thought about it. Never cared one way or the other. Dead is dead—who cares what they do with me after that? I sure won't.

I curl further into his body, taking his silence for fear, not knowing what to say, not wanting to set out false hope.

"The police are going to take me into protection. I don't know where they'll take me. They told me not to tell anyone," I whisper.

"It's for the best. This won't last forever."

"No, it won't. Not much longer now."

Silence falls again, heavy, smothering.

"I don't like not knowing where you are," he says finally.

"Best you don't. Lily—" Sudden tears stop me, visions of her dead in my bed blinding me. I feel as if I'll never close my eyes without seeing her gaping, slashed throat and empty eyes. It will forever flash before my closed eyes. I think about her laughter, drinking with me, whispering to Alex and me about cute men in the bar. Trying to coax me into a one-night stand with someone, just for fun. It was a fun night. I suppose it's good that she had fun, since it was her last night in this life.

Fuck.

Tears roll from my eyes, not just for her but for all of this.

By early afternoon, Doug has kissed me goodbye and handed over a new phone. When he found out that my old one had in fact been seized, he got my number transferred to a brand-new iPhone, refusing to let me pay for it. When pushed, the police told him there were images on the old phone that they needed, and it was also covered in blood. He also got me fresh clothes, having gone to Macy's to get me a few outfits and some other things. He forced me to make a list of what I needed, then showed up three hours later with two new duffel bags full of items for me to go into hiding with.

A young patrol officer arrives, and I'm taken off in the front seat of his patrol cruiser without knowing where I'm going. The drive takes over an hour before we pull into a Comfort Suites and I'm taken to room

112 on the first floor.

I expect an empty room when I get there, so I'm beyond surprised to walk in with my bags and find none other than Chief Mike Mitchell sitting at the table playing solitaire with the television off. His cowboy hat hangs on the back of the chair, and he doesn't even look up when we walk in.

"Shut the door" is all he says.

I say a silent prayer, hoping this man is not my company for the evening.

"Chief Mitchell, fancy seeing you here." I smile.

He glances up, tossing down an ace of spades. His green eyes betray his distaste for me despite the smile he flashes. "Yes, after the weekend you had, I expect it's good to be seeing anyone, isn't it?"

I swallow. Is that a joke? A dig about being alive on borrowed time? "Any day above ground is a great day, as they say," I offer.

He laughs, looking back down at his cards. "Yes indeed. Yes indeed." He tosses another card down and moves one. "So, let's have a chat."

I sit down, suddenly feeling very tired on top of annoyed with this idiot. I watch as he scoops up the cards while giving me a sideways look.

"It's a bit overdue, don't you think?" he asks.

"Yes, I do."

# CHAPTER TWENTY-FOUR

## THE LIST

"WHAT WOULD YOU LIKE FOR SUPPER, young lady?"

"Um, I don't even know."

"I'll get us something. Patrol can pick it up for us. Now, did you tell anyone where you were going?" He scribbles down a few things on a hotel notepad and hands it to the officer who drove me, who then leaves.

I raise an eyebrow. "No one told me. I had no clue where he was bringing me. Are you my company for the evening?"

He nods, leaning back with a sigh. "I am."

Ugh.

"Okay, so tell me about yourself."

I think the question surprises him, and I smile at his briefly blank expression. "Alrighty then. I'm fifty-six, divorced, and I have four grandchildren. I've been chief for twenty-seven years, and this is the first serial killer I've dealt with in this little town. I have caught my share of killers, however."

I nod. Somehow the divorce isn't much of a shock.

"What about you?"

"I'm soon to be divorced, no kids. You know the rest, I'm sure."

He nods. "Yeah, I know a bit. I've been following Small's investigation rather closely." He pulls a hefty file out of nowhere, laying it on the table with a slap. "Your lawyer friend came in and requested a copy of the case, correct?"

"Yes, I forgot all about it. Is that it?"

"It is. I thought we might take a look at it. What do you think?"

I stand up, eager to learn what's going on, stupidly optimistic that I might be able to see something they haven't after all this time.

"Hold on there, young lady. There's some gnarly stuff in here. You sure you're ready for this?"

"I woke up covered in blood next to a dead body yesterday." It's the only answer I offer.

Seeming to understand, he pulls the empty chair over and pats the seat, intending for me to sit down.

"Well, if it gets too much, say something."

Sitting down, I realize I'm holding my breath when he opens the folder, the first page being a form, and I release it. It looks like a statement. Chief Mitchell starts to sort the contents, one pile for what looks like statements, one for pictures, facedown, another and another. "This isn't everything, but it's all you would get anyway. There are boxes of evidence on this sick bastard. This is just the paper on it."

I nod, unsure of what to say, of my next move. He sets a paper in front of me. "This was a list Small made for his own purposes, but I pulled it anyway. These are the names of all the victims, the dates."

Elizabeth Malcom. Date of birth: October 6, 1987. Date of Death: May 1, 2017. Age thirty-two.

Stacy Witcom. Date of birth: December 23, 1995. Date of Death: August 30, 2017. Age twenty-four.

Shelby Patterson. Date of birth: July 3, 1998. Date of Death: January 7, 2018. Age twenty-one.

Gabriella Martinez. Date of birth: February 14, 1997. Date of Death: May 31, 2018. Age twenty-two.

Faith Carruthers. Date of birth: July 2, 1990. Date of Death: October 31, 2018. Age twenty-nine.

Angela Miller. Date of birth: November 18, 1999. Date of Death: February 6, 2019. Age twenty.

Maya Chavez. Date of birth: January 18, 1998. Date of Death: Unconfirmed

Lily Cohen. Date of birth: June 6, 1996. Date of Death: April 18, 2019. Age twenty-five.

I stare at the list, taking in the fact that Angela was only twenty. That my friend Lily is now on the list.

I mentally add my own name.

Wren Addison. Date of birth: September 22, 1993.

Date of Death: TBD. Age twenty-six.

"There are months between killings. I thought he said that—"

He shakes his head. "It is months, almost random. But he's been fucking with you since Angela Miller. We just didn't find her until weeks later. I think you were meant to be in Lily's place."

"You're the second person to tell me that," I whisper, touching the list.

There's no date of death next to Maya's name. "Was this one the one they found while I was in California? The one in the picture he sent me?" I touch her name.

"Yes. We haven't heard back from the medical examiner yet. She was stored for a while."

"He isn't consistent at all, is he?"

"No, he's not."

He pulls out pictures. "These are the women alive." Some are random snapshots, others professional images, a couple of selfies. All very pretty. Dark hair, light hair, same with the eyes. "They range from twenty to thirty-two and are all attractive. Professions are all over the place, nothing in common. We haven't figured out why he's choosing them, or why he chose you."

"Well, there has to be something. Isn't there always something?"

"Usually. And that's usually the key to unlocking the whole damn thing and catching him. The way you found Lily yesterday is how we found them all. Some freshly dead, some not. Some left where they died, others moved like Maya was. All slashed to ribbons, all but drained of blood. There are traces of fluids, so he's not using a condom, but we have nothing to compare the sample with. It's not in the database."

I look at the pictures of the women, studying them. I pause on Angela for too long. Hers is a selfie with a background you can't really pin down. The woman who stood on my porch and ruined my life.

"Was this one pregnant?" I ask, showing him her picture. "Angela Miller."

"Funny you should ask that." He shuffles papers. "Three of them were actually pregnant. All early term, a few weeks, maybe two or three months. It's possible they didn't even know."

I swallow. *Fuck.*

He pulls out what I assume is an autopsy report and scans it. "Angela Miller." He sucks his teeth as he reads. "Deceased was ten weeks pregnant at the time of death."

I inhale, holding it. Ricky lied. I'm not sure where the lie was. Maybe he was with her more than once or not when he said he was. I want to ask what the odds are that it was the killer's baby, but I don't think she would've risked showing up at my door to find Ricky if she hadn't been sure it was his. She was trying to track him down to make him responsible, and I assume, the killer probably found her shortly afterwards. I wish it was the killer's baby, but I guess

I'll never know. It wouldn't change anything anyway, I don't think. It must've been Ricky's, and now I stare at her image, remembering all the lies he told me with such convincing pain in his eyes. Begging me to believe him, pleading for trust and swearing his love to me.

Ricky's "she's crazy" holds less and less water as the chief slides the report over to me and I stare at the words. They hurt, a lot. My Ricky, his baby. He made a baby, a person, a child with someone who wasn't me.

Well, he's not my Ricky anymore. And whatever doubts I may have had lingering on giving him a shot are dead now. Funny how you have no real clue about someone, the person you choose to share your life with. He didn't act any differently; I had no idea he was with someone else. The man who cried and begged me to come home is the same one who looked me right in the eyes and lied to me.

I pass the report back to him. "That's strange, isn't it? That so many would be pregnant? If it was too early for them to know, then how could the killer know? It was weeks, months between killings. Could they be the killer's babies? Could he have done it during the initial rape?"

*Oh shit. What about me?* I feel the color drain from my face. *When was my last period?* I reach into my brain, thinking back. It's been a while, but with all the stress, I have no real idea of just how long it's been. Damn it.

"It's hard to know. It takes months to get labs like that back in these cases, and that's if there's enough to compare it to. Sometimes the samples we recover are just too small to use more than once. I know he did look into it, checked all their backgrounds, but nothing popped up. Most of them were single women, not in a serious relationship. Accidents happen."

"Most single women are pretty careful, and while accidents do happen, I'd say that's just not probable." I shake my head, glancing through the pictures while wondering which ones it was. Wondering if they knew. "Would it be possible to compare the babies to one another to see? With DNA I mean?"

"Maybe. I'll mention it to Small to put in the orders."

"Did any of these women report the harassment?"

He inhales and then exhales loudly. "None of the early ones did." He pulls out the picture of Shelby Patterson. "Until this one. She did call us a couple of times, said she was receiving harassing texts and phone calls. We don't know if the early ones were sexually assaulted initially like you were; none of them reported anything. The deaths were the same, but the harassment gets worse with each woman. He's escalating, as if something's irking him. He's not like any serial killer I've ever seen. He's only partly consistent—his method of murder, the biting—but there are more variables than most serial killers have."

"They're methodical."

"They are. Especially the ones who are sexually motivated."

"You don't think this is your everyday serial killer, do you?"

"I do not. This is something else. What, we just don't know."

"I know what Ricky told me, but can you answer a question?"

He eyes me without speaking.

"What's assumed, and what do you know for sure?"

He frowns. "What do you mean?"

"Ricky told me about sexual assault, bloodlust… all sorts of things. What's true?"

"I'm interested in what Ricky told you."

"I'm sure you are. You first."

He nods. "Fair enough. You have the list, the ages, the demographics. As far as the crimes, we have murder by stabbing and exsanguination. All had their throats cut. All were found with semen in or on the body. All were bitten and sexually assaulted before death. That's where the commonality ends. Shelby was the first to report harassment. None reported any sexual assault before the murder except you. Some of their phones were taken or broken at the crime scene. We did find some harassing images and messages to the later victims, but that doesn't mean the early ones weren't receiving anything."

"Easy to delete," I mutter.

"Exactly. He's left plenty of DNA behind, but we

have no match. No fingerprints though."

I frown. "That's strange, don't you think?"

"Yes, I do. Whoever this is, he's giving you worse than he gave any of the others. Now, tell me what Ricky told you."

I tell him about our conversation, watching his face. It reflects nothing, as is typical of any seasoned officer.

"That's interesting."

"Why is he telling me about bloodlust and sexual assault that way if you said you aren't sure?"

"We found cross contamination on the bodies later on, meaning we found DNA of one on the other. We weren't sure how it was happening. One theory was bloodlust, but there were other theories as well. It wasn't until you got that picture that we knew what might really be happening. I think Ricky is making some assumptions because he's too close and fancies himself a detective when he couldn't even hack patrol."

There was a time when I would have risen to his defense, but I know he's right. Ricky always did tend to be a little too cocky. A know-it-all.

I flip through the papers, pulling the statements toward me. The stack is thick.

"Those are from friends, family, coworkers, anyone who might have known anything at all. A little light reading for you."

I look up at him for a moment and note how he's staring at the file. Could it be that we just got off on the wrong foot? Maybe he's just someone who comes off like a dickhead, but when it comes down to it, he's not that bad. Not that I'm getting all lovey-dovey, but it's almost been like a pleasant conversation with him.

Almost.

"Thanks for going over this with me."

"You're welcome. I understand. I might not know what it's like to be on your side there, but I do understand." He shakes his head. "I think there's a reason for all this. A purpose besides his madness."

Seems to be. Now that I know more, I have the itch to call Doug and tell him, or tell Ricky that I know the truth. Maybe check on Alex.

"Hey, you said you can make my probation go away." I narrow my eyes at him.

He smiles like a man caught with his hand in the cookie jar. As if he forgot he said that to me. "Oh, I did, didn't I?"

I nod, taking the stack of statements to the sofa and wondering absently how much longer the food is going to take. "Yes, you did. You said if I work with you that you could help me."

"I'll see what I can do. It really is up to the judge, but with a good word from me and your PO, maybe it can be shortened, or you can at least get an occupational license so you can drive to work."

"That would be great. And I am friends with her, so I'll call her and tell her."

He nods, gathering the papers before reaching for the remote and the cards. I settle in on a small sofa, adjusting my pillows to start reading statements.

# CHAPTER TWENTY-FIVE

## HIDING

I READ MYSELF RIGHT TO SLEEP ON TOP of the blankets with the light and my shoes still on. When I wake up, the lights are out and the chief is still playing solitaire. My phone tells me that it's after midnight. I kick off my shoes, move the papers, and head for the small private bedroom just off the living space.

Only after changing do I look back at my phone. Missed calls and texts. Ricky has called me half a dozen times. His name on my screen makes me frown, but knowing it's just shitty to scare someone to death, I swallow my anger and dial his number.

"Hey, where are you?" he answers immediately, even though it's so late. He sounds wide awake.

"What do you want?" I yawn.

"I saw what happened on the damn news. Why didn't you tell me? I've been worried."

"The news? I didn't know it was on the news. I was in the hospital for shock, and then I got pulled into protective custody. The cops are sitting on me to keep me alive."

He breathes heavily into the phone. "Damn, babe. Where are you? Can I come see you?"

"No. And don't call me that." I stop short of unloading on him, yelling at him for the lies; I'm too tired to waste my breath. "I can't tell anyone where I am. They think he intended to kill me but found Lily there, so it was just bad luck for her."

"Wren—"

"Stop. I'm tired. You know I'm alive, I'm with a cop, so calm yourself."

"I'm the one who should be protecting you."

"If not for what you did, I never would have been alone in the first place."

The words shock even me after they come out of my mouth. Painful silence hangs for a beat, then two, then three.

"Wren, I—"

"I need to go. It's late. Bye." I hang up with tears in my eyes, eager to get off the phone before my voice breaks or before he says something to remind me of my feelings. I guess eventually it won't hurt anymore, or I'll be dead and won't care.

***

The chief is gone when I wake up the next morning.

In his place is a woman who looks to be in her midthirties, wearing khakis and a polo with a gun belt on her hip, her eyes glued to *Pawn Stars* on the TV screen. There's fresh coffee and a box of something on the counter from a donut shop.

"Morning." I smile, headed for the coffee. I lift the lid to find kolaches, a Texas breakfast staple.

"Morning, Mrs. Addison. I'm Officer Weyer, here for the day with you."

I nod, sipping hot coffee and munching on sausage and cheese wrapped in soft, warm sweet bread. "You really think you guys can protect me? How long are we going to do this? He's not just going to give up, you know."

She nods, turning dark blue eyes my way. I wonder if she's married, divorced, has kids. "I know we'll do our best. No one knows where we are that we know of, and we don't want to just turn you loose to be murdered. Not much in the way of options here. Detective Small has a team working around the clock on this case, hoping something will crack."

"Is he any closer than he was before?"

"I'm not sure. But the FBI has started calling. They might end up sending someone to assist him in the investigation. They caught wind that we had a serial killer, and they tend to step in when that happens."

"I see. Understandable, I suppose. Do you want some coffee or something?"

"No, had plenty, thanks."

I smile and return to my room, deciding to call Doug and tell him what the chief and I talked about yesterday, what I found out about Ricky and his dead homewrecker.

"So she *was* pregnant," he breathes.

"Yes. She was ten weeks. He said it had been months, and that she was crazy and wouldn't leave him alone. It must have been more recent, or maybe it didn't happen like he said at all."

"Maybe a short-term fling that got out of hand. If you know he cheated, what's the difference if you know the whole truth? Why compound it with more lies?"

"I don't know. I haven't confronted him with it. I'm not sure what the point would be. It won't fix anything, or bring her or that baby back. He obviously didn't love her. I saw how he looked at her. There was no love there."

"Maybe he's just protecting your feelings."

"Maybe he's just protecting himself." *Maybe he's just a pathological liar, and I'm a damn fool.*

He sighs into the phone. "I wish I could take you to lunch or something."

"I'm not a prisoner. I don't think I can do this for days and days or weeks. I have no idea what to do."

"Don't go rushing off into the dark now. There is a killer waiting for you, remember?"

"Maybe killing Lily was enough. Maybe he'll move on past me." Even as I say it, I know it's not the truth.

Now I'm a challenge.

"I guess it's possible, but you won't ever really know, will you?"

"No kidding. I'd spend all my days wondering if he's going to pop up until he's caught."

"They're going to catch him."

"There are plenty of serial killers who never got caught."

"I know, but from what you said, he's not a normal serial killer. Something is off about him."

"I think so, yes. I don't know, but I have been doing research off and on over these last few weeks, and he's not methodical. He's not following a true pattern. He's not fully predictable. There must be a reason. The only thing consistent is his method of murder. Chief Mitchell agreed with me. He thinks something else is going on."

He sighs. "Yes, I noticed that. I'd like to see those statements."

"Maybe we can meet up. I have the file here."

"I want to see you. I've been thinking about you, Wren."

I smile, warmed. "Not just about all this killing stuff, I take it?"

He breathes in and out deeply. "No, not at all. I keep thinking about the conference and then in my office. I want you again. I want to take you away somewhere." His voice softens at the end, like he's offering me the world.

I lean into the phone a bit, falling back onto my pillows. "Where would we go?"

"Anywhere you want."

"Anywhere?"

"Yes."

He likes me. Maybe even cares for me. A sudden reality makes me frown, takes the gentle tone out of my voice. "Don't get attached to me, not until we know if I'll live to return the feelings."

"I don't want to protect myself. I want to feel it, feel you. I want to. Just let me, okay?"

"I might die."

There's a brief silence before he says, "I know. But I'd rather risk it."

He's the first to say that. The first to finally face the reality and not feed me bullshit and say I'll live when we all know the odds aren't in my favor. It's a shock, like ice water or a slap, but I appreciate it. His honesty, the frankness.

"You don't want to hurt like that, surely."

"Of course not, but if I have to choose between a short time with you or walking away from something that I really like, then I choose the risk. I'd rather have you for a short while and hope I get to keep you than not have you at all."

The words stir something inside me that I haven't felt since I was dating Ricky. But back then I was just a teenager, and young puppy love grew into more adult feelings as the years went by. Feeling the stirrings as an adult is an entirely different experience.

"Doug—"

"It's okay, don't say anything. Just trust that I know what I'm doing. I'm not a kid."

I smile. Indeed he's not. He's no twentysomething who has no clue about relationships. He very likely knows more than I do about these things. "Okay. You make me smile. Not an easy thing to do right now."

He chuckles, and I hear the grin in his voice. "Good, that makes me happy. If I can do anything for you, please let me know."

"I need a dress for Lily's funeral. I don't think I can get back into my place for a while."

"Done. It was a twelve, right?"

"Twelve should do it. Size seven shoes, please? You don't mind? I'll pay you back."

"No, you won't. I'll take care of it."

I grin and agree with him. We chat for a while; with nothing better to do, I'm in no rush to get off the phone.

Afterward, I call Alex, who tells me that, due to our friendship, another PO should be taking over my case. The idea makes me panic. She assures me that she'll make sure it's someone who will do me right, but I don't see how she can promise that. Then she tells me that, considering the state I was in when they took me to the hospital, she's thrilled to hear from me. She promises to be at Lily's funeral and to take me out for dinner as soon as I'm free to go.

I check in with the detective—no new developments.

No one else has died. He tells me that a press release was issued, and the media has been calling and asking for me down at the station, wanting to talk to me. I swallow, not sure if releasing anything to the media was the best idea. No new survivors have come from it, and I'm not so certain that it really helped.

But then again, it might save someone in the long run. If I die, women will know about the SMS Killer and they'll come forward in the future. Maybe then my death wouldn't be in vain.

# CHAPTER TWENTY-SIX

## GOODBYE

BY THE FIFTH DAY IN THIS SUITE, I'M ready to pull my hair out. The same four cops come and go; the chief hasn't come back. I ask them if I can have a break, get out of here, but they all say no. It's for the best. For my own good. Like I'm a grounded child and someone is trying to teach me a valuable lesson.

I groan my protest and end up back in my room, watching mindless daytime TV and calling my friends and whining to them. Doug gets my dress but ends up having to take it all to the police station, where one of my guards picks it up and brings it to me. I'm presented with a nice garment bag and shoes still in the box. I've never bought a dress that comes in a garment bag before. Makes me wonder how much he spent, if he's trying to impress me or just spoil me a little with something nice.

After a shower, I slip the dress over my head. It fits

perfectly, just snug enough to show off curves but still be terribly classy, especially with the long sleeves. I smile as I curl and fluff my hair, checking myself in the mirror, but then I frown at my reflection.

Lily is dead. I was supposed to be dead in her place. It was supposed to be her dressing for *my* funeral, crying at *my* wake.

I inhale sharply, reaching for my makeup. Somber, muted colors, nude lipstick. A bit of perfume. I wish I had a silver necklace and earrings to put on.

I exit the bathroom, finding the officer in dress uniform. He glances at me, then back to his phone as I slip on new low-heeled leather shoes. Tasteful, comfortable, surely expensive.

I'll see almost everyone today—Doug, Alex, people from the office. I doubt Ricky will attend, not having known Lily. A bit of a relief not to have to worry about seeing him today.

Time to say goodbye to a life ended way too short.

It's a long, reflective ride to the church. Funerals always make one think of death, the end of everything, what you should and shouldn't be doing. But here lately, I do that anyway. If I had any affairs, I would be forced to get them in order. But I don't, so Ricky can deal with it since he's still my legal beneficiary. I have to accept that there isn't anything I can do. I can't predict the future, and I'm past freaking out. There is no peace, but the anger seems to be fading. Maybe it was seeing Lily like that that did it, finally broke me.

I feel as if I lost a bit of my fight that morning.

The funeral is in this large cathedral-like Catholic church downtown. Lily was a popular girl, happy, outgoing, but nothing that would stir a turnout like this one. We get a block from the church and come to a complete stop. There's a ton of traffic, car after car, people walking past us in dark clothes, down the sidewalk and toward the church. People I've never seen, dozens upon dozens.

"This is insane," I mutter, pulling my phone out of my bag and calling Doug.

"Hey, gorgeous. You doing okay this morning?"

"I'm all right, but what's with this crowd?"

"The media has been talking about the murder. The funeral arrangements were all over the news all week. They came down to the office to try to get an interview. Carl, the receptionist, talked to them and ended up getting suspended for it because he went on and on about the firm and Lily's position and her job. He's not fired, but I think they're just going to leave him hanging for a bit to teach him to keep his mouth shut."

My mouth drops open. "Are you serious? Damn, that's ridiculous."

"It's the media for you. They call them vultures for a good reason. I'm already inside. I've got a seat saved for you."

"How did you get through the traffic?"

"I parked and walked."

"I wonder if they'll let me just walk up there."

"You're not in custody. You can do what you want."

True, but people always hesitate to disobey the police. Well, most people do. "I guess so. I mean, it's not like anything will happen here, right? He does everything at night while I'm sleeping. He only showed up during the day that one time at Ricky's."

"Tell them you're meeting me, that you'll find them after or something. It's a funeral, for Christ's sake. You need to be with your friends at a time like this, not under armed guard."

I turn to the officer. He's young and looks pretty irked that we've been sitting for so long. "Officer, I can get out here and walk. My friend is inside. I can meet you afterward."

He frowns at me. "You're supposed to stay with me."

"Yes, but I don't have to. Besides, nothing will happen here. There are too many people. I'll meet up with you later, right?"

He narrows his eyes at me but pulls out a card and scribbles his number on it with the pen from his front pocket. "Okay then. I'll be here. Don't hesitate to contact me, got it?"

I nod, sliding the card into my purse. "For sure. Thanks."

I get out of the car and shut the door, looking around before putting the phone back to my ear. My heels click on the asphalt, heat from the street radiating upward as I walk toward the sidewalk, slipping into the crowd.

"I'm back. He let me out."

"I don't want to lose my seat. I'm in the middle. Count back from the front—" I hear muttered counting. "—nine rows. I'll be on that one."

"Got it. Keep your phone on you, just in case."

Ten minutes later, I'm squeezing past strangers, my eyes locked on Doug. I want to ask him how many of these people could have known her, how many are rubberneckers, how many want to be able to take a church selfie and say they attended the funeral for the eighth victim of the SMS Killer, but I bite it back.

I fall into a warm hug. He smells of the same cologne, his body hot and hard, soothing me. Being alone for a week with strange cops has taken a toll on me, made me a touch stir-crazy. My mom used to call it cabin fever when I was a kid, bugging her when there were long stretches of bad weather that kept me indoors for too many days. Being with him is like stretching my legs out in the warm summer sun after a long winter.

He laces his fingers with mine and presses his lips to my forehead. I wonder if Alex is here, where she is. Lost in this crowd, no doubt.

After we sit down, I text her. She answers quickly and says she's parking. I didn't think to tell Doug to save her a seat, but she says that's no big deal and she'll meet up with us later, maybe graveside.

I've been known to skip the graveside service at funerals before, but for this one I plan to stay. I have to. Lily seemed like such a happy, carefree person.

Who knows what was really going on in her head, but externally she was bright and bubbling, a real outgoing personality. She drew me out when I really didn't want to be, and I usually ended up enjoying myself in spite of it all.

The eulogy is painful, as they always are. I cry silently, dabbing my eyes with the tissues I remembered to pack. Doug holds my hand or gives me one of those one-arm shoulder hugs throughout the service.

"This procession is going to take ages," I mutter as the service ends.

"Yep. Ride with me, and then maybe we can sneak off for a while."

When I look up, his eyes are twinkling. "After the graveside service?"

He nods. "Yeah."

"Maybe. We'll see."

He smiles, and I do too, despite where we are. I'm glad to feel a moment of something besides black dread.

As predicted, the procession and the graveside service take ages. The funeral ends up lasting the bulk of the day.

When it's over, I scan the crowd for the officer I came with, but I don't see him. "Let's take off. I don't want to go back to the hotel right now." I scoot closer to Doug.

He grabs my hand, nodding. "Okay. It's going to take time to get through this mess."

When we reach the parking area, I realize the media is here. Their vans are set up anywhere there is room, and right off the bat I see half a dozen reporters. Some are talking to people; others are talking to their cameras. I hold my breath, hoping we can slip by unseen, melt into the crowd.

Doug follows my gaze and then pulls me away, but it's too little, too late. I'm suddenly surrounded by three reporters out of nowhere, different from the six I saw a moment ago.

I stop walking, ambushed. Nowhere else to go.

"Aren't you Wren Addison?"

"You were there at the time of death, weren't you?"

"Can you tell us what you saw?"

"Do you feel responsible for her murder?"

"Is the killer still after you?"

"Why do you think he didn't kill you both that night?"

They continue to throw question after question at me, and all I can do is gulp, swallowing only air and saliva. My mouth goes dry as I look over at Doug. I don't know what to do, what to say. How much to give away. What's too much?

I try to think for a moment. What did the police say? What did they hold back?

"Yes, I am her. Wren Addison. Yes, I was with her," I squeak.

"What can you tell us? Can you speak up?"

More of them arrive, and suddenly I can't see

past them. I'm separated from Doug, and their close proximity makes me feel short of breath. I try to back away from the microphones and phones in my face, but I hit a parked car. It's hot and hard against my back, a wall caging me in with the lions in front of me.

"Back off! Back off!" the officer I arrived with orders. He shoots me a dirty look, but I don't know what he's silently scolding me for. Maybe for leaving the church without him, or for getting into this cluster of media.

"Wren, tell us about that night. Did you hear him? Did you—"

"She's not free to talk," the officer cuts in. "Let her out."

I take a look around, seeing Doug. With a glance at the officer, I head for Doug, taking his hand and rushing to vanish between the cars. The officer's blocked by the media, and this time I'm grateful for them as he strains to see where I've gone. By the time he escapes, I'm in Doug's front seat and looking over my shoulder to see if any of the officers there for security saw me.

If they did, they aren't following me. I suppose it's silly to worry. I'm not a fugitive, after all. They're likely thinking I'm stupid at this point, and if I want to get murdered, then whatever.

"Where are we going? Can we eat? I'm starving." I haven't had anything since breakfast, and it's past three in the afternoon.

"We can go to my house and cook something.

How's that?"

I nod. "Okay. Do you cook?"

"Yes, ma'am. I enjoy cooking. What about you? Do you cook?"

I shrug. "More for necessity than enjoyment. Ricky was more the cook. Funny how you cook too."

"How is that going with him?"

I groan. "It's not. I haven't called him or anything. I don't want to talk to him. I'll get a lawyer when all this is over."

"It'll end soon."

The words loom large. "One way or another." I sigh.

"I didn't mean—"

"I know what you meant. It's fine. The only thing I can do is accept it."

"Don't give up the fight, Wren, please. I only just found you."

I don't know what to say. His words suggest something I don't know if my mind can take. My heart swells, strangely hopeful, warmed, happy.

Confused, guilty, married.

Married legally. Not emotionally. There's a big difference.

He pulls into a decent-sized driveway, and I realize I've never seen his house before. He lives in a nice townhome that looks like it was built within the last ten years. Dark red brick, roses in bloom.

I follow him inside. Stairs to the left, hallway to the living area, which has a floor-to-ceiling window. It's lovely. Cream-colored carpet, dark leather furniture, wall-mounted TV. His sneakers sit by the fireplace in a heap, a basket of laundry close by that looks like it was folded but never put away. A coffee cup sits on the bar.

It's not perfect. Neat but comfortable. A place where I could be content in my bare feet, wrapped in a blanket on the couch.

"I like it." I smile.

"I was hoping." He tosses his keys on the bar and walks around it into a galley kitchen, opening the fridge. "I have steak, or we can make burgers or pasta. I could even whip up chicken-fried chicken." He smiles over his shoulder, closing the freezer and opening the fridge. He takes out a bottle of red wine. "Would you like some?"

"Please." Home cooking sounds divine, and fun. I kick off my heels and leave my bag in a chair, joining him in the kitchen. "Chicken-fried chicken comes with gravy and mashed potatoes, right?"

He laughs, nodding. "Of course. Anything else is sinful, right? I have chicken already thawed in the fridge. You want to start on the potatoes? They're in the pantry."

I locate a half-full bag of red potatoes and wash them as he starts on the chicken. I used to help Ricky cook sometimes. I've just never been into it on my own; the times I do it, it's for fun, because I want to, like when bonding with someone over food.

He takes off his jacket, rolls up his sleeves, and

takes off his tie. I'll probably get the dress dirty, but it's okay. A little flour never ruined anything.

We laugh and he tells me stories of crazy court cases, his childhood, his two brothers, and growing up. Tales of putting himself through law school, his first wife and their divorce. I ask him questions here and there, wanting to know what I'm getting myself into. Of course, it was over ten years ago, but some things don't really change.

Soon we're sitting at a small table with heaping plates of hot food, homemade from scratch. It's pleasant. Occasionally I remember what brought me here, but only for a moment.

After dinner, we're too full to consider dessert, so we decide to curl up in front of the TV for a movie. Snuggled up under a blanket, I move into him and am so cozy and warm that I start to get sleepy. He notices and gives me an elbow.

"Hey now, you gonna fall asleep on me?"

"No," I mumble, scooting closer when he puts an arm around me. I settle into his shoulder, refocusing my eyes on the movie. "I've never fallen asleep on a date before." I yawn.

"I don't know if that's good or bad." He laughs before kissing my ear. "I guess you're comfortable."

"I'm perfect."

"Damn right you are," he growls.

I smile, turning and offering my mouth to him.

He kisses me softly at first, but it ends up urgent and hungry, his hands in my hair, hips pressing into mine. I whimper my approval as clothes start to come off, and we end up having slow, sensual sex on the couch.

Afterward, I'm led by the hand to his bedroom, my naked, sated body wrapped in the throw from the couch. The room is like the rest of the house, imperfect but nice. A dark navy and white quilt is on the half-made bed. It looks as if it was tossed up over the mattress in an attempt to make it look made, but failing a bit. I smile at him.

"Will you stay?" he asks me softly, his voice barely above a whisper. "Tonight, I mean. Or do you need to go?"

I sit on the bed, shaking my head. "Where would I go? Back to the police? They would yell at me."

"They should. I should. But since I'm complicit in your escape, I won't." He sits beside me, wrapping an arm around me. "I could get used to you."

"Probably best you hold off on that."

He sighs, and I can't blame him for his frustration. I should pretend that it's not what it is, that it's normal and nothing is wrong. That I won't have nightmares, or wake up dead any day now. But I can't. It's just so close now, the end of this. I can feel it.

"You make me forget," I murmur, so quietly that even I struggle to hear it.

"Do I?"

I nod. "Yes." All the hell, the blood, the death. The

pictures and taunting. The questions. "You make me feel normal. It's been a while, even before. I didn't feel anything but miserable after I left him. Just hurt and dejected. I still have that feeling, I guess, but I'm so fed up and angry that I don't care."

"I dealt with that during my divorce too. At least there aren't kids. Mine were pretty much grown, so they weren't an issue for us. Will he fight you in court?"

"I don't know. I've heard that you never really know what will happen during something like this."

"Very true. People turn into different creatures when they're scared and hurting."

"No shit," I mumble. "What time is it?"

"Around ten."

"Can you grab my phone so I can check in?"

He stands up, and while he's gone, I toss the throw over the footboard and crawl into bed. The sheets are cool and feel nice, soft, high thread count.

A yawn overtakes me just as he reenters the room. "Here you go."

I text Alex, Detective Small, and, after a moment's hesitation, Ricky. Then I put the phone in airplane mode, setting it aside, not wanting to chat with anyone. After the harassment, I don't much look at my phone anymore. I'm absent from social media altogether, and my email is full of media requests, so I've been ignoring that too. "Thanks. I don't want anyone thinking I'm dead just yet."

He turns the lights out before he crawls into bed and

curls up behind me. With his arm around my waist, it doesn't take long before I'm asleep.

# CHAPTER TWENTY-SEVEN

## GAME CHANGER

THE NEXT DAY AFTER I WAKE, I HAVE a choice. Do I go back to the protective custody of the police, or do I just live, take what might be the last days I have and enjoy them?

But what kind of enjoyment will I find knowing someone might be right behind me? Therein is the dilemma.

I look up and find Doug watching me over his coffee cup with a frown. "What are you thinking about?" he asks.

"Nothing."

He raises an eyebrow at me. "Don't 'nothing' me. Tell me."

I sip on the coffee for a minute, thinking. "I just don't know what to do. The smart thing would be to go beg the police to hide me, right? But the thought just…." I groan. The scent of the coffee suddenly makes my stomach roll, and I set the cup down. The nausea is unusual, but perhaps my stomach is just finally feeling the stress the rest of me feels. The scent wafts up and curls around me, hitting my nose, making it worse.

"I see the problem. Live or hide. Hide or die."

"There is no right answer," I mutter, frowning at the gaggy feeling that rises in my throat. "Damn, I don't feel so good."

I get up from the table, telling him that I need a bit of fresh air to settle my stomach before stepping outside. As I pace up and down the driveway, taking in the perfect morning and the clear sky, I realize there is one thing I need to do, and it scares me almost more than dying does.

In the end, I decide to go back to my life. When I call the detective, I can hear the frown and fatherly tone as he tells me that I'm making a mistake, but I just shrug and say I can't hide forever. I give my notice at my apartment, unable to even look at the inside of it one more time knowing what I know. I can't unsee her dead body, all that blood, but I don't want to move in with Doug even to hide.

I end up letting him help me out with a hotel room in the middle of town. He insists on getting me a nice suite, not knowing how long I'll need it, not caring how much it costs. I offer him money; he rolls his eyes at me. The room is nice, with a pretty little sitting area and a balcony that overlooks the bay. I tell the police where I am, then talk to the manager and give him the gist of my situation, telling him only a handful of people will know where I am, and if anyone not on the list asks for me, he needs to call the cops right away. The police decide that stationing an officer in the lobby is in my best interest, just in case, and I'm left feeling semi special to have my own pet officer whenever I need him.

The chief calls me and tells me that I have a hearing on Thursday with the judge to get my occupational license, allowing me to drive myself to work once more. The idea of having that small piece of my freedom back elates me. It's silly, but right now I have to think about the small things.

Days go by, and my life starts to feel almost normal. I go to work, I make the hearing and get that small chunk of freedom back, and Doug comes by every evening. Alex pops in from time to time. I even meet my new probation officer. He's young and pretty damn cute. Alex sits with us in our first meeting to bring him up to speed on me. I suspect she did it so she might influence him to go easy on me, since we're friends now. She even got the chief to write a letter for my file, making me look even better, hoping it might help to shorten my time in the end.

It really does feel like things are falling into place. I haven't heard anything from the killer, not a peep. The media are still after me, but I don't expect that to stop anytime soon.

During the day I work, and on the weekend, I spend

part of the day apartment hunting. I go with Alex and Doug to pack up my things, throwing out much of what was in my bedroom and preparing the rest to move or store since I don't know what will become of me from one day to the next.

The nausea still comes and goes, and I realize that I'll have to bite the bullet sooner rather than later. I grit my teeth and call Alex, needing a woman with me, wishing Lily were around to call. She's probably been through this before.

"Hey, how are you?" There's a smile in her voice when she answers the phone.

I pace the floor of my suite's balcony. "Hey, I was wondering if I can meet you. I need to…." I take a deep breath. "I need to take a pregnancy test."

Her gasp is audible. "What? Oh shit, honey! Where do you want to meet?"

"I don't know. I'm going to walk to the drugstore to get a test. Maybe you can pick me up and we can go take it?"

"Um, sure." She pauses a bit too long, and I wonder if I'm making her uncomfortable.

"If you don't want to, it's okay. I'm just pretty freaked out about this. It can only mean one thing, and I need the company."

"No, no, I can come. It's fine. Let me know where to meet you."

After a few minutes, I hang up, grab my purse, and exit the hotel. I walk four blocks to the drugstore, wishing I didn't need to go in, thinking about what other things I might grab so it looks like the test is a second thought and not the only reason I came to the store. Like it matters if this seventeen-year-old cashier is judging me, a grown woman. I laugh at the thought of adding condoms and lube to the transaction with the test just to see his face.

In the end, I buy the test, some makeup, a bag of chips, and a soda. By the time I'm done, Alex is texting me that she's in the parking lot.

"Do you want to just go back to the hotel?" she asks me when I get in her car.

"I guess so."

The short ride is silent. It isn't until we get to the elevator that she asks, "What if you are? Whose is it?"

"Well, it can't be Ricky's. That hasn't happened. Doug had a vasectomy, so it's not his. That only leaves one person." I can't even say it. The idea makes me feel dizzy.

"Who?"

"The killer." The words sound loud as the elevator opens.

She turns to me, wide-eyed. "What? Are you sure?"

She looks as scared as I feel. "I don't know. Maybe I'm not. I can't believe I'm even speculating. But I haven't touched Ricky, and Doug and I just started a few weeks ago, so there isn't anyone else."

"Shit," she whispers, following me into the hall. "Damn, what if you are? What would you do?"

I shrug, unlocking the door, trying to be cool, not freak out.

Pregnant with a killer's baby. DNA… inherited illness… raising a psychopath—too many questions race through my head. Then again, the kid might turn out totally normal and be nothing like him. Or I might survive one killer only to die at the hands of my own child. "I don't know."

She sits on the love seat and plays with her hair, watching me as she twirls it around and weaves it between her fingers. I stand in the middle of the room, fish the box out of the bag, and set the bag aside on the side table. I can't remember the last time I took one of these things—maybe right out of high school. I'd been on birth control pills since then until they started making me hormonal, right before Ricky and I broke up.

I rip open the box on my way to the bathroom. Pulling out both tests, I shut the door and toss the directions into the trash with the box. As I open the pink-and-white foil, my hands start to shake.

Maybe it won't be so bad. If it comes out positive, I can be a mom. I always knew that someday I would be one, though I didn't imagine doing it alone. I thought it would be us, me and Ricky.

I blow out a breath, holding the stick in my hand. Is my life about to change? I've had a bit too much of that recently.

I inhale, exhale, and pee on the damn thing. I set it

aside and try not to stare, but I do.

Waiting. Waiting.

One line, then two. Bright, bold pink. Positive. A fast positive too.

Tears fill my eyes as my hand goes to my stomach. A baby. It must be his baby. It can't be anyone else's. Bastard.

I toss the test, knowing I'll take the second one the next time I pee. I leave it out on the counter with the rest of my crap and exit the bathroom, trembling.

I don't find Alex where I left her. Instead, she's on the balcony, gripping the railing and half leaning over it. Her knuckles are white, her eyes worried when she glances at me when the sliding door announces my arrival. Turning, she leans on the rail and crosses her arms over her chest. "Well?"

I wish there was some place to sit, suddenly feeling heavy. "Positive."

The color of her face changes before my eyes, from sun-kissed bronze to slightly paler. "Fuck. What will you do? Abortion?"

I hadn't thought that far ahead. "I don't know. I don't think so. If anything, adoption. I don't think I can kill my own baby. But the father being a killer... I just don't know what to think. Even if the kid is normal, I wonder how I would feel about it all."

"What, like taking your anger out on him? Every time you see the kid, you see the guy who wanted to kill you?"

I nod. "Something like that."

"I'd have an abortion. Carrying around a rapist's baby, that's fucked up." She shakes her head, turns and looks over the bay. The water is choppy; it's windy today. A few brave souls wade in the too-cold water, though not many.

"I don't think I can do that. God, what will Ricky and Doug say?" I put a hand to my forehead.

"You sure it's not Ricky's?"

"We haven't had sex in around six months."

"Will he be upset?"

"Probably. He wanted me to come home. He wants me back."

"How do you feel about him seeing other people?"

What a strange question. I shrug it off, more worried about other things. "I don't give a damn. He started before I left anyway." I laugh painfully.

Doug might decide to break up with me. I don't even know how I feel about having a serious relationship with anyone. I like him, he's great, but to settle down again so soon? I don't know about that. Backing off might be something to think about, but breaking up is… I just don't know.

I don't know anything right now. My brain is all fuzzy. It would be simpler to just go home, forgive Ricky, and just suck it up. I miss him.

And just like that, I want to tell Ricky we can start over, that I want to try again.

"I want to go home," I mutter, my voice breaking.

She turns. "What do you mean?"

"Ricky. I want Ricky." Tears roll down my face like a child crying for its mother.

She frowns. "You can't. You know what he did. He cheated on you, got someone pregnant, and he's still lying about it."

I nod. "I know. But I miss him. He was mine once. I miss that."

She shakes her head. "You're just scared."

"No shit, Sherlock."

We both laugh, but my heart isn't in it, and judging by the look on her face, neither is hers.

"I got to go," she says abruptly. "I'm meeting someone for dinner. Call me, okay?"

"Sure."

I walk her out, not sure what my next move is. Closing the door behind her, I find myself picking up my phone, dialing without thinking.

# CHAPTER TWENTY-EIGHT

## TRUTH

"HEY." HIS VOICE IS DEEP, MAYBE EVEN sad. I blink, unsure of what to say, why I called.

"Hey, are you busy?" I roll my eyes at myself. Silly to be nervous.

"Not really. Just doing some work outside. I could use a break. How are you doing? How is that hotel?"

"It's nice, but it's not home."

"Come home."

His offer is instant, soft. I ache inside to say yes, but I don't know what the right thing to do is. I probably am just hurting, reaching out for something comfortable to ease the pain. I know it's wrong, not really safe for my heart.

"I can't. Can we meet up or something?"

"I'm running in the marathon in the morning. Why don't you meet me for that? You can cheer me on, and then we can go do something."

"Oh, really? I didn't know you were running. I guess I can do that. What time?"

"Race starts at nine."

"Okay."

"Wren… I miss you."

I close my eyes, not sure if I'm trying to hold the words in or block them out. I wish he'd been better, loved me more. I wish I'd been enough for him, though I'm inclined to believe that no woman would be enough for someone like Ricky. He's a selfish bastard, but I loved him once. I hope he loved me in return, even just a little.

"Me too," I admit, regretting saying it out loud after it leaves my mouth.

We chat for a few minutes, just small talk. I catch him up on everything except today's news. I can't make myself say it out loud yet. Not to him.

He doesn't tell me much—nothing new there. I don't ask, not really caring. The sound of him on the phone is comforting enough.

When I hang up, I'm still confused, still alone.

When Doug arrives with dinner, I watch a movie with him, eat with him, but I don't tell him. I'm not in the mood to fool around, so he leaves around ten and goes home after kissing me good night.

I sleep and dream of babies and murder and being fat and round with pregnancy. It's not peaceful or restful in the least.

It's early when I get up. I dress in capris and a loose

tunic-style hoodie in a deep purple. It's thin cotton, so I won't get hot. I slip on shoes and head out, wondering what this day will bring and what the hell I'm doing.

I meet Ricky before the race. He smiles at me, kisses my cheek, tells me he's glad to see me. I can see that it's true, and it makes me feel better that I came. I sip the spiced tea I stopped to get since coffee makes me feel sick, and he heads off, leaving me to find a place to watch the race.

It's somewhere at the 3k mark of the 5k when it happens. Ricky runs into someone, then stumbles and falls. He holds his ankle, gritting his teeth in pain as the medics help him off the track and into the back of an ambulance to be checked out.

I stand with him, watching them feel his ankle, note the swelling. They say it's sprained and wrap it for him, telling him to go to the doctor to get it looked at. I know he won't.

"Are you okay?" I hear a familiar voice ask. Turning, I frown in confusion. Alex is behind me, leaning into the ambulance. "Is he all right? I saw him fall."

I turn to Ricky, his expression telling me more than anything: the slack-jawed surprise and then the flush that rises to his cheeks, the frown, the anger flashing behind his eyes. "What are you doing here?" he growls.

"I came to watch the race," she offers, only glancing at me.

"What's going on?" I ask.

"Nothing," they both chime in unison.

Nothing, my ass. I feel the tension between them, the pissed-off vibe he's putting out. Alex moves toward him, a gentle hand on his foot. He jerks it away, snapping, "Don't touch me."

She blinks, looking almost tearful.

What the fuck is this?

"Did something happen between you two?" Stepping between them, I grip Alex by the arm. "Why are you here? Why are you touching him?"

She pulls away, eyes darting between us. "Nothing happened. I'm just worried because he's your husband, that's all."

I smell the lie. I can almost taste it. I look at Ricky, who's watching me. "Do you have to tell me something?"

He nods. "Yeah, but not here. Let's go home and we can talk there."

I turn back to Alex, who's gripping the handle to her shoulder bag, looking like she wants to say something. She doesn't, just backs off, watching as I offer Ricky a hand, grabbing the crutches the medics gave him and assisting him to his feet.

I drive his car back, not caring that I'm breaking the law. All I can think about is asking him if he slept with my friend. The way she looked at him was off, not normal for a woman who met a man only once. Not the gaze a friend of a friend has. There was more to it. And his anger, it was instant.

I settle him on the couch, pillows under his foot,

Advil in his stomach, ice pack, the works. Only then do I sit down, but I wait. I refuse to beg for answers, not this time.

He blows out a breath. "There's something you don't know about Alex, I think."

"Clearly."

"She called me like a week ago. We got to talking. I don't even know how she got my number, but we clicked, and I agreed to meet her for dinner."

I grip the arms of the chair, but I don't say anything. I keep my face set like stone, refusing to give him the satisfaction of showing my emotions.

"We went to eat, and she kissed me. I invited her here. We started to fool around, but then I reached down and… I felt a dick. She's a fucking man."

I balk, stunned. Not at the fact that he was ready to fuck my friend—that will come later. "What? No way. Alex is not a man."

He nods. "Yes, she is. I reached under her skirt and she had a full set. Hand full of dick, balls, everything. Got hard in my hand, I swear to God. I was shocked. I had no idea. I lost my mind; he started to cry. It was all fucked up."

"Alex can't be a man. Come on." I shake my head. "This is unbelievable. She's so… feminine. She's prettier than I am. She has breasts, for God's sake."

"Breasts are fake. She—he—is a man."

I feel like the wind's been knocked out of me. "But how could she think you were going to just…?" I shake my head, suddenly finding it very funny. I start to laugh, and he frowns. "She even sounds like a woman. I don't believe this."

"I don't know. I guess he was hoping that I might be convinced or something. It's not funny."

"Yes, it is."

I start to argue, but then the front door opens and we both turn to see Alex, tears on her face and a huge knife in her hand.

She winks at me. "Hey there, sexy."

# CHAPTER TWENTY-NINE

## FOUND

*I CAN'T MOVE. I'M FROZEN. THE SNAPCHAT* flashes to my mind—**Hey there, Sexy.**

No. *No.* Just a coincidence, has to be.

I feel like I'm watching a movie of someone else's life as I lock eyes with my friend, my PO, standing in the doorway staring at me.

Alex shuts the door and moves the blade from one hand to the other. "So, what are we talking about?" She smiles with tears still falling from her eyes.

"Why do you have a knife?" I whisper.

"Oh, honey, I think you know, don't you? Did you tell him yet?"

"Tell him what?" *This can't be. It isn't. No. No, no, no.*

"That you're pregnant with my baby." She cocks her head to one side.

Ricky sits up. "What?"

Oh God, I am. Alex's baby. Fuck me, who would have ever guessed? I'm shaking so bad, my eyes on the knife.

"It's not you. It can't be you." My voice is weak. I can't even make myself stand up to back away, run out. Anything. "You're my friend. We hang out. It doesn't make sense."

She moves toward Ricky and sits on the arm of the couch behind his head. He's sitting up but hasn't moved. I feel what's left of the blood draining from my face, knowing he hasn't put it together.

"It's me. It's always been me." She holds her arms out, grinning. "Ta-da! What a shock, right? Alex, the SMS Killer." She bows, eyeing me. "That was the beauty of it, wasn't it? You and me together the entire time. Turning to me to talk when all the time it was me. I knew you'd never guess. Your face, it's even more priceless than I imagined it." She grins at us both, proud as a peacock.

"What the fuck?" Ricky tries to stand, but she presses the clean metal to the flesh of his neck. "You're the killer? The one who—"

"Yes. Now, Ricky, my dear, my love. You know so much more than you've let on, don't you? You saw all those women, the ones I killed, and you had to know."

I stand up, eyes on the knife. He's breathing heavy, trying to back away with nowhere to go. She runs her free hand through his hair. "I don't understand."

She looks to me. "You didn't put it together either.

I really thought one of you would."

"Put what together?" I ask. I watch Ricky's eyes, wide, staring at me, begging me to do something.

"Honey, lie down." She pats the pillow on the couch, pointing the knife at him. Ricky lies down without argument.

Alex lets out an exasperated sigh. She shifts so she's straddling behind his head, the knife in her right hand, her left stroking his hair as she stares down at him with soft eyes.

She loves him.

*What the fuck?*

"I met Ricky in college. He was my roommate, all four years."

Ricky's eyes widen further, recognition in them. "What? No way. No. Way." He tries to shake his head, then winces. "My roommate was Alex Gomez."

She leans forward so he can see her face. "Yep. That's me. We were good friends, but I couldn't ever get up the nerve to tell you. I was too scared back then to be me; I did it in secret. It wasn't easy to come out back then, you know? But I knew deep down that when Ricky found out, he would love me like I loved him. The way he looked at me told me everything I needed to know. He's my soul mate, and soul mates always find a way to be together."

She takes in a deep breath. "After college I just couldn't ever let him go. We met before he ever knew you, Wren. I had him first. But as the time went by, our friendship fell away, and he met you and got married. You stole him from me. At first I was just going to kill you and take him back, but then I realized when I saw him with that first woman that you weren't the one for him."

I see it then, the realization. Ricky suddenly understands. He closes his eyes and swears. "Fuck."

"Ah, there it is. You know."

"But I wasn't with all those women. I don't know them all."

"You did, you just don't remember. I saw how you looked at them, and I knew they would be in your bed if I didn't act. I caught many of them early, before you got to them."

Then it sinks in. I fall back in the chair, heavy with the truth. I reach back into my memory, trying to think on how I missed it. Him cheating on me so many times. "Oh my God."

"I'm sorry. I was a shitty husband." Tears flow from his eyes as he turns back to Alex. "Please don't kill me."

"Honey, I came to kill her. But I'm not finished." She looks up. "You see, I realized the weakness he had for women, so I became one for him. Implants, hormones, the works. I know you liked it. I could tell. I saw you checking me out."

I swallow because my mouth is going dry. She runs her hands through Ricky's hair lovingly.

My eyes widen. "So all those women, they were…

they were pregnant with his babies? Like Angela was?"

She nods. "Yeah, I think so. I couldn't have that, the permanent connection keeping him away from me. He's mine, you see. Always has been. I think on some level you always knew, right, Ricky?"

I plead with him silently to play along, to not let his macho indignation get in the way of his life.

"Yeah, I guess so," Ricky says. "We were always sort of close." He holds my eyes.

"Then you two started talking about divorce, and I wondered if I would be able to let Wren live. But I knew deep down that she would always be between us, so…." Alex shrugs.

I start to cry. This is what I fought too hard to avoid. What I hid from, and the killer still found me. I guess somehow I knew it would happen, but it's nothing like I expected. Nothing. "So you're not really a serial killer, then."

"Well, in the technical sense, I am. It completely threw them off the trail, didn't it?" She laughs, eyes glittering but still somehow sad. "I loved it. Reading all that bullshit into everything I did to you, to them. Now I get my moment, the epic ending where the killer explains his motivations and you and lover boy here plot your escape. But this time it won't end like that. I think you know, don't you?"

She cocks her head, waiting for my answer.

"No, it won't. But if you're gay, then why did you rape me? "

She rolls her eyes. "I'm not gay. I love everyone, men and women. But the assault, yes, that was partly to throw you all off, and for punishment. You especially had to be punished for taking what didn't belong to you. Ricky wasn't paying attention to me, so I had to do it. The worst way to violate a woman is to rape her. You both had to be taught a lesson. You for stealing him, and him for ignoring me."

She takes in a deep breath. "But my Ricky is really a bit of a manwhore, and I know he won't ever stop. I've really been thinking about that. Woman after woman, it hurt so much. Every time I saw you kiss one of them, sneak off with them, fuck them in a car, it hurt me. I can imagine she feels the same." She nods to me. "But she didn't know about all them. You don't deserve him, you know. You didn't pay attention to him. You didn't love him enough to see what he was doing. I did."

My blood rushes in my ears. I have to keep her talking, but I don't know what to do. If I move, she'll slit Ricky's throat, I just know it. She obviously has no issue with killing a pregnant woman, so I doubt that will save me.

This might be it. She has the advantage, and I have nothing. Not a single thing within arm's reach to use, no secret moves. This isn't a movie. This is reality, and sometimes the good guy dies at the end.

I feel a weight on my chest for a moment, knowing I probably only have a few minutes. Alex has the upper hand, seems she always did. I was hanging out with my attacker, letting her into my house, telling her my secrets. She even knew when I was in police protection, though she didn't know where. All the time I wasted, all the moments of my life flash in my mind—memories of my mom being the most prominent. Not to mention the fact that the man I married never really loved me the way he said he did. He got several women pregnant, cheated on me again and again.

"Look at her. She's getting mad," Alex whispers in Ricky's ear. She pulls the knife from his throat but keeps it close. "Who do you think she's angrier at, me or you?"

Ricky blinks and tears fill his eyes. I'm so done with his tears, but I don't want him to die. "Are you going to kill us?" I ask quietly.

Alex grins, a frighteningly happy smile. Psychotic, for sure. "Oh, I can't tell you everything, now can I?"

"Why did you do things the way you did? Toying with me? With all the women? Why not just kill them?"

"That would be too easy. I really enjoyed the game. You've been my favorite. It was total coincidence that I ended up as your PO, by the way. I didn't plan that. It just worked out perfectly when I saw your file come across my desk. Made you even easier to track, since you had to keep me informed. When we got to be friends, it was simply divine intervention. The look on your face when I walked in here and you realized who I was? Totally worth the wait."

My heart beats so fast I feel a bit dizzy. Likely my

blood pressure is skyrocketing. "But, Alex, you got me pregnant. I don't think you planned that."

She frowns. "No, I didn't. That was a mistake."

"You sexually assaulted me three times. I thought you would have used a condom."

She shakes her head. "No, but I suppose hindsight is 20/20, eh?"

I watch, terrified, as Alex gets up, moves around, and straddles Ricky's hips. She faces him, knife in hand, and her eyes go sad. I can't breathe. I gasp, unable to catch a deep breath, unable to fill my lungs as I cry.

"Please don't kill my wife," Ricky whispers, looking up into Alex's face. "I'll do anything."

Alex leans forward, tears in her own eyes, which confuses me. "Baby, hush." She kisses Ricky on the mouth, savoring it, nuzzling him before pulling back. "You know that you and I, we'll be together forever. Tell me you love me."

"I love you, Alex." Ricky is sobbing. We're all crying now. "Please, I'll go with you, just leave her alone."

Ricky looks at me. "Wren, I'm sorry. I wasn't the man you deserved, but I did... I do..." He stops short of saying "I love you," fearing his captor—our captor. "I'll always regret what I did."

I suck in a breath on a sob, unable to find words. I just stare, horrified, blood rushing in my ears, unsure of what to do. I'm trapped.

"You won't, not for long," Alex says, glancing at me. "Wren, it was fun, wasn't it?"

I nod, not knowing how else to respond.

"Take care of my kid, okay? Don't tell him about me."

Before I can open my mouth, she leans forward, grabs Ricky by the hair, and uses the blade to open his throat, leaving Ricky wide-eyed and cutting off his scream with a wet-sounding gurgle. Blood rushes from the wound, spurting across Alex, the couch, everything.

I don't even have time to scream before Alex looks at me one last time, winks, and cuts her own throat in the same fashion.

I never imagined anyone would have the strength to cut through the pain. I hear myself screaming, but it sounds so far away to my own ears as the life fades in Ricky's eyes, as Alex falls forward on top of him, both dead in a minute.

The room dims. I struggle to stand, but my legs won't hold me, and I fear maybe she drugged me. My last thought is that she tricked me as I collapse and the world fades.

\* \* \*

I wake in the hospital, alive and anything but well. I'm sleepy, and the nurse tells me it's the medication, that when I wake, I start screaming and they've been forced to keep me knocked out for days. I don't remember any of this.

I look around and realize I'm not in a regular hospital. When I ask the nurse, she tells me without a smile or any warmth that I've been admitted to the neurological and psychological unit at the hospital.

The mental ward.

Fuck my life.

I start to cry, looking for my phone. It's not here. There is no phone. For a horrifying moment, I wonder if any of it was real, if maybe I've been here the entire time and I've totally lost it. Maybe this is just a rare moment of lucidity for me and I'll slip back into my delusion. When I ask, she assures me that it's real. It did happen. Ricky is dead, along with Alex. The case has been all over the news. Detective Small has apparently been waiting for me to be able to make my statement all this time.

After another few days, I'm released, and I finally remember that I'm pregnant. They confirmed it at the hospital, though they didn't tell me until they felt I could handle the news.

A week goes by before I can talk to the detective, and it's a struggle. It takes me days to tell him what happened. But they close the case, saying the evidence supports my account of the events that took place.

I pay a service to clean the house and then put it up for sale, fully furnished. I can't stomach going inside.

Now, three months later, I sit in my new apartment with my swollen stomach, baby kicking, eating toast with peanut butter on it alongside warm tea with milk and sugar. It took me a long time to decide, but I'm keeping the baby. It's a girl. I can't decide between Abigail or Olivia for her name. She won't ever know who her father was. Never. I have my doubts, as I rub my stomach and my baby girl kicks me, wondering if I'll be a good mom or if this damaged me beyond repair. The doctor says I'm not too far gone, so I hope she's right.

As for Doug and I, we ended up staying good friends. He understood when I told him I can't mentally handle a relationship. I can barely handle a friendship. My psychologist says it'll be a while, but eventually with a lot of work, I should be able to trust someone again.

The doctor tells me that someday I'll forgive them, Ricky and Alex, and it'll help me find peace. When she said that, I laughed, long and loud, and told her to go fuck off with her forgiveness bullshit.

I hope the two of them are happy together in Hell. Maybe they were soul mates after all.

THE END

Thanks for reading *Carnal Knowledge*. I do hope you enjoyed my story. I appreciate your help in spreading the word, including telling a friend. Before you go, it would mean so much to me if you would take a few minutes to write a review and share how you feel about my story so others may find my work. Reviews really do help readers find books. Please leave a review on your favorite book site.

Don't miss out on New Releases, Exclusive Giveaways, and much more!

JOIN MY NEWSLETTER
WWW.RACHAELTAMAYOWRITES.COM/CONTACTME

LIKE ME ON FACEBOOK:
WWW.FACEBOOK.COM/RACHAELTAMAYOWRITES

JOIN MY READER GROUP:
WWW.FACEBOOK.COM/THERTASYLUM/

FOLLOW ME ON TWITTER:
@RTAMAYO2004

FOLLOW ME ON PINTEREST:
WWW.PINTEREST.COM/RACHAELTWRITES

Follow me on Goodreads:
/www.goodreads.com/author/show/15251093.
Rachael_Tamayo

Follow me on BookBub:
/www.bookbub.com/authors/rachael-tamayo

Visit my website for my current booklist:
www.RachaelTamayowrites.com

I'd love to hear from you directly, too. Please feel free to email me at Rtamayo@ rachaeltamayowrites.com or check out my website www.rachaeltamayowrites.com for updates.

# ABOUT THE AUTHOR

Rachael Tamayo is a former 911 emergency operator and police dispatcher. After twelve years in those dark depths, she's gained a unique insight into mental illness, human behavior, and the general darkness of humanity that she likes to weave into her books. A formerly exclusive romance author, she tried her hand at thrillers in her award-winning novel Crazy Love and loved it so much that she decided not to turn back. Born and raised in Texas, Rachael lives in the Houston area with her husband of almost fifteen years and their two small children.

# ACKNOWLEDGMENTS

First I would like to thank my husband. Thanks for being my sounding board, for listening to me drone on and on about plots and characters and books, endlessly scheming out loud to you. Thanks for the endless support and for being so excited to read the next book.

Thank you to my editor, Kristin. I love you and always look forward to your thoughts and comments. Thanks for putting up with me when I'm frustrated with the books!

Thank you to Maggie, Andrea, and Cynthia. For being there, for listening, for helping me out when I come to you begging for a sounding board. I love you guys!

And most of all, to the readers. I love you all, and I look forward to your emails and comments. It's you guys who keep me going. I wouldn't be here without you—really. So thank you so much for reading!

# ABOUT THE PUBLISHER

As Hot Tree Publishing's first imprint branch, Tangled Tree Publishing aims to bring darker, twisted, more tangled reads to its readers. Established in 2015, they have seen rousing success as a rising publishing house in the industry motivated by their enthusiasm and keen eye for talent. Driving them is their passion for the written word of all genres, but with Tangled Tree Publishing, they're embarking on a whole new adventure with words of mystery, suspense, crime, and thrillers.

Join the growing Hot Tree Group family of authors, promoters, editors, and readers. Become a part of not just a company but an actual family by submitting your manuscript to Tangled Tree Publishing. Know that they will put your interests and book first, and that your voice and brand will always be at the forefront of everything they do.

For more details, head to
WWW.TANGLEDTREEPUBLISHING.COM.